"Why did yo...

Mira swung her lovely legs off of the bed in a motion as graceful as it was revealing. Her voice was low but strong with the tension in her, like the suppressed sounds made by a stalking cat. "I felt bad about the way things went between us at my place. I came to set them right, Sam, baby."

"They're all right," Durell said tonelessly.

A smile came to her pouting lips and she moved onto the arm of his chair. The straw of the chair made punished, snapping sounds under her light body as she leaned toward him.

"We could make them better," she said.

"You're using your sex like an iron mace, Mira."

She made an amused sound deep in her throat, but there was something like anger in her smoky eyes.

Then she pressed her breasts against his chest and put her lips close to his, and Durell felt the fuses blow on his self-control as she said, "But didn't you know? Sex has always been a weapon. Come, let's make beautiful, wonderful war."

Fawcett Gold Medal Books in the Assignment Series:

Assignment Sheba

Will B. Aarons

A FAWCETT GOLD MEDAL BOOK

Fawcett Publications, Inc., Greenwich, Connecticut

ASSIGNMENT SHEBA

Copyright © 1976 by Fawcett Publications, Inc.

ISBN 0-449-13696-5

Printed in the United States of America

10   9   8   7   6   5   4   3   2   1

Durell was stuffing his shoes into a locker at the Villa d'Este, an exclusive club on the shore of the Red Sea, when the first explosion bounced dust from the sill of an iron-barred window.

The two other men in the locker room froze, waiting for their senses to decipher the sound. Round-eyed, they looked at each other; one in his fifties, his graying mustache curling into the corners of his slightly parted lips; the other, in his twenties, tanned and hard, his thumbs hooked into a scanty yellow bathing suit he had pulled halfway up his thighs. Father and son, Durell had guessed. Italian. Their *patois* told him both had been reared in Eritrea, descendants of immigrants who had come when it still was a colony of Italy.

Durell reflectively recognized the crump of the hand grenade, followed by two more in rapid succession.

He dug for his snub-nosed .38 S&W. It was behind his shoes, tangled in his pants where he had rolled it for safekeeping. Too late. The pounding of boots came from the hallway. He left the gun, jumped a scrubbed wooden bench, and headed for a door that was the only avenue of escape. His mind and body had been honed for survival by more years of danger than he cared to remember as chief field agent for K Section, the trouble-shooting branch of the CIA.

The angry rattle of submachine guns mingled with screams from the restaurant and bar. It had to be the ELF, Durell thought He did not want to get caught in Ethiopia's war.

He had his own.

Durell leaped to the blind side of the door as a boot crashed into it from the outside. It burst inward, swinging to cover him against the concrete wall. He heard the young Italian scream, *"No! Per piacere! Please!"* and was deafened by the slamming sound of a submachine gun. The acrid smell of smokeless powder filled the air. The young Italian threw his arms toward the ceiling and toppled onto his back as slugs tore sodden blue holes across his chest and jarred into the row of lockers behind him. The bullets blasted away half of the elder Italian's high forehead, spraying blood and tissue glimmering into the barred sunrays. He pitched forward, his look of astonishment unchanged.

Durell waited.

The terrorist started into the room and Durell saw the snout of his Arab-supplied Russian AK47 assault rifle and gave it a practiced yank with both hands. The guerrilla lurched forward off balance; Durell smashed him in the Adam's apple with the hard edge of his palm. The gunman's eyes rolled and he gagged and grappled at his throat, buckling to the floor. Durell thrust his knee hard into the bloated face, felt the nose go mushy. The blow snapped the man onto his back with a broken neck.

Others would be coming.

The racket of guns and slaughter came from everywhere in the building and palm-shaded grounds outside.

Clad only in red bathing briefs, Durell ran down the narrow corridor bisecting the building. His shoulders prickled as he thought of bullets hammering into his back. He tried a door on his right. It opened into a closet stacked with cans of chlorine and pool equipment.

Anger wrenched the pit of his stomach. He quelled it. Anger was too expensive in his profession. Survival went to the cool-headed, the calculating. If you survived long enough, the characteristics became ingrained. You became a master at figuring the odds under pressure, like his Grandpa Jonathan, one of the last Mississippi River gamblers. He had raised Durell on his old sidewheel riverboat, *Trois Belles*, beached on Louisiana's Bayou Pêché Rouge. By the time Durell left for Yale, the old man had taught him all he knew about hunting and being hunted, about the flaws and strengths of men. After Yale had come K Section, every mission a no-limit poker game with survival the stakes. Durell's mind combined a gam-

6

bler's instinct with a computer's cold mastery of probabilities.

But in the Villa d'Este that computer was missing a vital bit of information.

Only the previous afternoon, Durell had been working in Ankara. He had been sent there to reorganize K Section's network in the aftermath of political dissension between Turkey and the U.S. that had threatened to kill U.S. intelligence efforts right down to their roots.

The mysterious General Dickinson McFee, gray little chief of K Section, had met him on a bench under a lemon tree, his ever-present blackthorn walking stick held loosely between his knees.

"We're in a hurry, Samuel," he said. "Ineyu Worota, our Ethiopian Central, has been missing for forty-six hours. You've seen the satellite photograph. If it shows what we fear, the world has entered a calamitous era; perhaps the *final* era of civilization. Ineyu disappeared about the time the photo was taken. He may very well have information pertaining to it—if he is not dead. You must find out what the photo means, Samuel; you must bring Ineyu back to us. Sheba, our employee in Asmara, has an important lead."

"I'd like to see a floor plan of the Villa d'Este, sir," Durell said.

"It is not readily available."

"This is basic; I need those plans to memorize. We could arrange for Sheba to drop them in Asmara, before I go down to the coast."

"Every minute counts. There is no time for further arrangements. We must *move.*"

"I'm in no hurry to die. She's asking me to go into a strange building and take off my clothes. What if something happens?"

"We would miss you sorely, Cajun." McFee seldom used Durell's code name.

"But you could do without me."

"We could. You have to go."

"I could turn down the assignment."

"Don't talk nonsense, my boy. You've never turned

7

down a mission. Will you now, merely because you don't know your way around a bathhouse? Your plane leaves in half an hour."

The "bathhouse" was turning into a Byzantine nightmare.

A second door led to the kitchen. Two terrified cooks hid beneath a work table. Durell ran past them and jerked open another door just as guns hammered from the far end of the room. Milky water squirted from holes in a stainless steel kettle of simmering pasta. It hit the hot burners and sputtered into steam. Plaster stung Durell's face as a bullet drilled into the wall half an inch from his ear.

He slammed the door closed behind him, muffling yells of pursuit. Open French-style doors beckoned from across a wide, carpeted hallway. He sprang swiftly through the exit and onto a saffron beach. He was a tall, muscular man in excellent physical condition, and he was not breathing hard. He had plenty of speed left, but he could not outrun the bullets he expected to be spraying around him any second.

The Ethiopian sun struck at him like a dragon, fiery and blinding.

Bathers ran in either direction, far down the beach. Seagulls scolded and fought over their picnic lunches. At a nearby pier, power cruisers and sailboats were casting off their moorings in frantic confusion.

Durell glanced over his shoulder without breaking stride and saw the nearby nude, strangely soft-looking bodies of victims lying on the lawn around the swimming pool. In the far distance, beyond the whitewashed walls of the club, the dusty blue escarpment of the great Rift Valley wavered through rising heat waves like a troubled curtain. Nothing but rocks and sand stretched away from the club's grassy compound.

Or the Red Sea.

Dhows of fishermen and pearl divers worked the neck of water between Durell and a barren island of the Dahlac group. The island shimmered on the sea like a hot rock. Durell figured it at a quarter of a mile.

He ran to the end of the pier and dived into the tepid water.

He swam outward beneath the surface. His locked breath rang in his ears. When it felt as if his chest would crack open, he nosed above the water. Shouts came from the beach. They sounded hollow, lost in the vastness of sea and desert. He glimpsed back and saw a man on the shore whip aside a white tunic, revealing camouflage fatigues and a submachine gun.

The water around him coughed spumes of spray; he felt something sock his left shoulder and the muscles just above the collarbone went numb.

He dived.

Above him he saw bullets plow paths of bubbles in the lucent water, making a sizzling noise. The feeling was coming back in his shoulder. It burned as salt probed the wound. He seemed to have the full use of his arm. His lungs ached for oxygen.

He carefully raised his head out of the water again. A volley of slugs immediately plopped into the swell six feet to his right. He looked back. Now three of the terrorists were taking turns firing at him. They stood abreast, laughing. The scorching wind tore at flames and thin gray smoke rising from the club building behind them.

He ducked beneath the surface once more. He wondered how much further he could go like this before becoming exhausted. The chrysolite waters pressed back, coiled around his arms and legs, pulling him down toward the bottom where schools of jeweled fish sparkled among the rocks. A man of ordinary endurance would have died there, muffled from life-giving air by six feet of lazily shifting liquid. He would have thought, "too far," and let the water into his tortured lungs, accepting a moment of agony for final rest in the warm, lulling depths. But Durell's mental discipline pressed him beyond that point. When he hastily arched back to the surface, his limbs were dead weights. He breathed in great watery gusts. He strangled, fought for control, only half heard the distant stutter of guns. He had moved beyond their accurate range, but the bullets still were deadly. They splattered over a wide area now, like gravel thrown into a pond.

9

A concussion hit him in the chest and stomach.

Durell heard shouts ahead of him.

The guerrillas were firing rifle grenades at pleasure craft that had begun milling among the fishing dhows, their operators drawn to the danger line by curiosity or the promise of thrills. The boats began to scatter.

Durell felt his last hope of salvation was going with them.

He could not get his breath. He choked, fought to keep from drowning. The shoulder wound had taken its toll of his strength. He laid his face in the water and tried to rest while floating.

Through the firing and explosions, he heard the thrumming of a powerful engine. He lifted his head, but could hardly see. His vision was blurred by pearl droplets; the salt water stung his dark blue eyes.

A motor launch glided toward him through the geysers.

A woman stood at the gunwale. Her chocolate hair was worn in a superb Afro; sparks of sunlight played on the soft curls. She wore the merest suggestion of a black bikini around her slender hips. Its strings were almost overtaxed by her full, taut breasts. Her pouting lips frowned. Her wide-set almond eyes were grim.

Pressed against her naked shoulder was the stock of a hunting rifle. She aimed at Durell and fired. He tried to dive as the boat coasted closer. Water seared his trachea, his chest shook with spasms. He had no strength left.

The girl rammed another round into the rifle's chamber.

Durell had only a second to think that it should end this way after so many dangerous alleys and lonely nights.

She fired again.

Then there was nothing.

2

At 4 a.m. a coverlet of still fog lay over

Washington, D. C. It swallowed the echoes of a jet rumbling away from National Airport and shed iridescent dew on sleeping bags of youths slumbering on the Mall. The city slept, but lights glowed here and there in the mist. They came from a few windows in the Pentagon, the White House and K Section headquarters at No. 20 Annapolis Street. In such neutral centers reposed the consciousness of the nation, awake even in the dead hours, listening, relaying, commanding.

Sometimes General McFee spent the night at his narrow limestone house on Connecticut Avenue, but tonight he had secluded himself behind the bulletproof windows and sophisticated alarm devices of his office-apartment on the top floor of the K Section building. A buzzer sounded from the candlestick table of Hitchcock design next to his bed. McFee's hand found the telephone receiver immediately in the dark room. "Yes?"

"General, sir? I'm sorry to awaken you, sir . . ."

"Yes, yes?" McFee never slept deeply. He spent his nights in a twilight state, his body at rest, but the gates of his mind open. Its thoughts flowed from pool to pool, streams of water poured onto a dry street, seeking gravity, making surprise turns and unexpected connections.

"Q communication, sir, Asmara, Ethiopia."

McFee tightened his grip on the receiver. Asmara meant Sam Durell. The Q designation got top priority treatment. Its urgent transmission superseded all other activities in the worldwide relay network K Section had diligently built up over the years. Q stood for trouble.

"Read it," McFee said.

"Cajun dead. Eritrean Liberation Front raid near Massawa, approximately 200 hours EST. Appears non-prejudicial."

"Where's the body?" McFee demanded. The flesh paled beneath his manicured fingernails as he squeezed the telephone.

"Body?"

"Query Sheba. I want a full report. Get an eyewitness account out of her. I want it within eight hours. And where is Sam Durell's body!"

"Yes, SIR!"

McFee replaced the receiver, his hand trembling slightly. *Non-prejudicial?* The term really meant accidental. That was impossible. McFee would pit Durell against the best intelligence agents in the world: none was more skillful or professional. Yet Sheba—or her informants—expected K Section to believe Durell had been killed by third-rate terrorists.

Someone was lying.

They would sweat before he was through, McFee thought.

He turned on the bedside light, swung his short, wiry legs off of the bed and thrust his arms into a gray dressing robe. He almost never allowed his mind to swerve from its orderly, objective grasp. Now, as he paced the floor behind the steel door of his apartment, he impatiently tried to pull his thoughts together.

He had lost many agents. It was a price one paid. But Samuel . . .

McFee sat before the cold fireplace in his living room. He recalled the time he had surreptitiously left through its chimney to put himself—presumably with the Pilgrim Papers—at the mercy of the evil Madame Hung. He had known that Durell would follow his trail, and that Durell would triumph.

He had staked his life on it.

They had quarreled from time to time. McFee had even threatened Durell—there had been that occasion in Washington's Rock Creek Park. But the threats had been meant only to guide Durell in doing what had to be done.

McFee paced, a little moth-gray figure. He turned his blackthorn walking stick around in his hands. It was a deadly instrument; a pistol in its handle, poison needle in its tip; in its shaft a thermite bomb and other lethal gad-

12

gets cooked up by the boys in the basement laboratory. How useless such a weapon was when he could not close with the enemy. He was confined by the nature of his position to administrative tasks while men, good men, hunted and were hunted in places like Paysandu, Damba, Mosul and Omdurman.

He had sent them to do it, to live or die according to their skill and luck. Some said—and McFee did nothing to discourage the rumor—that he had no feelings.

McFee's gray eyes became almost colorless.

Cajun's luck had run out.

They had known the results of the computer printout. Durell's survival factor stood at the incredibly low .8021 on a scale of ten.

McFee had asked him to take over as chief of Analysis and Synthesis only six months previously, after Durell had returned from an affair in Tanzania that added two more angry scars to his body.

Durell had suggested Hal Jamison instead. "But I want you," McFee had insisted. "You've taken enough risks in the field. There comes a time in every man's career . . ."

"I'll work at what I do best until the numbers catch up with me, sir. I won't take it."

"You will, if I order it."

"If you order it, don't ask me to renew my contract."

The Russian KGB had placed a red tab on Durell's file; so had Peking's dreaded Black House. The tabs marked him for assassination. Countless free-lancers wanting to make a mark for themselves and professionals living under a cloud because Durell had damaged or ruined their careers waited only for the right place and opportune moment to kill him.

"People all over the world want your head on a pike, Samuel. You can't leave us! you'd be as good as dead."

"I've learned a lot about staying alive."

"No education can beat the odds forever. At least think about it."

Durell had said nothing.

Now McFee wished he had pressed the matter further. He swung the blackthorn walking stick and made a sound like a batter fanning a fastball. He could easily crush a man's skull with the weapon. He tossed it onto his rumpled bed, took a heavy pipe with a bent stem from his desk. He packed it with his special mixture and lighted it with a silver butane lighter, watching the smoke evaporate in the currents of air-conditioning chilling his quarters.

The thing now, he thought, was whether to disseminate the report of Durell's death. His mind had focused again. It made him feel better.

Point A: As far as K Section is concerned, there is no corpse.

That could change momentarily, of course. But until it did, Sam Durell was not dead to K Section. If no body was ever found, an agent remained immortal in K Section files. Never had a missing agent's dossier been double-lined. No matter what an eyewitness said. Men had been missing before and had turned up. McFee remembered the case of Ian McAllaster. He had been gone twenty-seven months. Two trained agents had sworn he had been blown to bits near Canton. Charley Fretz had been in limbo even longer. Nearly six years. He had been clobbered by a Russian tank shell fragment in Budapest. Had amnesia. There were other examples.

Point B: K Section had taken a beating recently from small-minded, publicity-oriented politicians. Congressional hearings, supposed to have been secret, but leaked to the press, had endangered half a dozen operations and scores of agents.

In that environment, the loss of Durell—a blow to morale in any case—could be disastrous, McFee thought. Of course, the agency would recover, but this was a bad time for such a thing to happen.

Conclusion: Withhold word until Durell's death could be confirmed.

Then would be time enough. Men all over the world, unknown and unsung in their hazardous occupation, could wait a few hours or days to raise a glass and share a memory of Sam Durell.

3

Durell awakened with a start, tried to raise himself on an elbow, felt a pulsing ache in his shoulder and fell back. A hair rug prickled his skin. He lay for a second with his eyes closed. Dizziness washed him back and forth.

He was aware that someone was using a rough cloth to wipe the sweat from his forehead and temples, where his thick black hair showed traces of gray. The smell of spices and woodsmoke stung his nostrils. His mouth tasted of bile. His tongue was sticky, swollen with thirst.

The rush of a jet battered his ears, then he felt the earth shiver and heard angry concussions in the distance.

Durell licked his lips and opened his eyes again. Through a shifting haze, he saw a small, fawn-colored face surrounded by long, rusty-gold hair, its wide-set eyes the color of quicksilver beneath a spring blue sky.

"You have been ill. I am Deste Giroud." She spoke in English, but she was robed in the customary Ethiopian *shamma* of homespun cotton.

Durell struggled to pick up his splintered thoughts. He saw over him a thatch roof blackened by the smoke of cooking fires. Sunlight glared from a square doorway, the only opening in the stone *tukul*. Durell winced and looked away to see a dusky woman bent over a cooking pot. She grinned and nodded at him, making clucking sounds. Her cheeks were freckled with small ashes from the stone firehole.

The ground quivered with a series of detonations. Artillery fire, Durell thought.

Deste put a gourd to his lips. It held rainwater. The water smelled slightly of a stone cistern where it had been stored. Durell held a sip on his tongue. It felt cool and good. He rinsed his mouth and spat the water onto the dirt floor. Then he drank the rest of the water in the gourd.

He felt for the .38 instinctively. His hand slid across his chest, then down to the waistband of his bathing suit. Then he remembered leaving it in the locker with his clothes and passport.

Things began to come back.

Sheba—he was to have met her on the beach near the boat dock. She would recognize him as an American wearing red bathing trunks. As a countersign, she would flash a metal locker key tab stamped with the numeral 51. He would show her his locker tab, bearing the number 52. It all had been arranged.

Except for the ELF.

Durell cursed the foul-up.

No one had suspected that the ELF would hit the Villa d'Este at that very hour. In fact, the ELF was so random in its activities that the Villa d'Este might as easily have escaped forever. The Eritrean Liberation Front had been raising hell for years and seldom did big damage, a bomb here, a shootout there. The typical work of a guerrilla movement that could not mature, living off of the scraps of harassment rather than the red meat of strategic victories. But lately it had gained strength against a confused and divided military government that had overthrown the 3,000-year-old monarchy.

Durell had been told to conceal his presence from the new regime. Because of the talkative nature of diplomats, that meant from the U.S. embassy as well. The old emperor had been friendly with the U.S., but the military rulers had not made their position clear and relations were strained. K Section was not to do anything that would tip them the wrong way.

Durell's vision had cleared now.

The girl bent over him and fanned the blue flies from his face. He wondered: Did that lovely face belong to Sheba?

She did not reply to the question in his eyes.

From the bones of dreams still rattling in his brain, Durell knew he had been delirious. He might have mentioned Ineyu. If so, it could lead to the death of a good central. He thought he remembered calling out something about the RT12, the geophysical research satellite, but he could not be sure.

"Did I talk much?" he asked.

"Very little."

"How little?"

Deste pursed her small apricot lips and thought for a moment, as if trying to recall.

She is working too hard at it, Durell thought.

Then she said, "You mentioned a General McFee. Was he at the Villa d'Este? I hope he was not injured."

"What else?"

"Sheba. Yes, Sheba. Is she your lover?"

"The job's open," he said.

"I'm surprised." She smiled.

There must have been more. She was not leveling with him. His dark blue eyes became darker as he waited.

She sighed. "That's all," she said. As if to change the topic, she said, "You lost much blood. Your shoulder there." She pointed to a plaster over the torn flesh where the bullet had struck. It was a superficial wound, but his weakness told him it had bled profusely.

He kept his eyes on the girl's face as she dabbed at the sweat on his cheeks.

She looked so innocent.

It was a most lethal quality.

"Where are we?" he asked.

"A fisherman's house. They helped me carry you here. I pulled you from the water. I shamed them; they didn't want to help. I called them cowards. I told them they were afraid of the *feranji* even when he was helpless and naked. They said, 'What good is he to us? He has nothing worth stealing.' " She laughed and her small, perfect teeth gleamed in the low light.

That fit, Durell thought. The fisherpeople were Tigrinyan, one of the two principal tribes of Ethiopia. But across the strait from their islands, wild Denakil tribesmen roamed the salty, lava-strewn desert. They paid allegiance only to the rifle and sword. They were among the world's fiercest people. It was the custom for a young warrior to present the scrotum of an enemy to his proposed bride.

Over the ages, the fisherpeople had found it necessary to adopt the Denakils' savage ways to some extent in order to survive against them. Durell probably owed his life to the fact that he had left his pistol in the locker. The Denakils had been known to kill a man for his gun—the Tigrinyans might be as bloodthirsty.

Durell remembered the girl firing at him from the speedboat, her hair aflame with the sunlight.

"Did you see what happened?" he asked.

"I was in a dhow, watching the man dive for pearls—I am a naturalist. I thought the woman had killed you. She looked very frightened. Why did she shoot you?"

"I'll find out. She missed. I got this from the ELF." He touched the plaster and winced.

"Did you know her?"

"No."

It must have been Sheba, Durell thought. She had been surprised by the ELF raid, too. But it had given her an excellent chance to pick him off. She had been just a bit too hasty. She would have used the rifle on him even if there had been no raid. Maybe the high-velocity slug would have knocked him over as he stood waiting by the boat pier or maybe later, after they had made contact and she thought his guard was relaxed.

She could still be out there, somewhere. She might have seen his rescue.

The rifle's deadly reach was long.

Alarm gnawed through Durell's guts, a hot, ravenous worm. He suppressed it, tried to relax the muscles tightening on his long frame. He needed rest before anything.

"You are a naturalist?" he asked.

"I was educated at the Sorbonne in Paris. I am half Ethiopian. My father was French. He was an attaché with the embassy in Addis Ababa when he met my mother. She was flown to Paris in a courier plane to give birth to me."

Durell brushed the sweat from his eyes. It glistened all over the hard ridges of his body. He was in one of the hottest spots in the world, he reflected. It was a few miles south of Massawa, the main port of Ethiopia's northernmost province of Eritrea. The Italians had built Massawa into a modern port in the 1930s, during the latter days of their fifty-year colonial hold on Eritrea. In 1935 the Fascists had launched their conquest of Ethiopia from Eritrea with war supplies brought from Italy via Massawa, their mustard gas and bombs taking a ghastly toll of the poorly armed tribesmen. The British had kicked the Fascists out in 1941. The U.N. had administered Eritrea for many years, but it was annexed by Ethiopia with its consent in 1962. But the ELF was not buying that combination—it wanted an independent Eritrea. And it did not much care how it got it, Durell thought.

Whoever controlled Eritrea's 500 miles of Red Sea coastline would have their grasp on the throat of one of the world's strategic waterways.

Again the sand beneath Durell shuddered to distant, surly explosions. He crawled to the doorway of the *tukul.* The sunlight clawed at his eyes. The heat, which seldom went below one hundred degrees even at night, pounced humidly, smothering him. It was late afternoon.

The copper sea stretched 900 miles north to the troubled Gulf of Suez and 200 miles east to the shores of Saudi Arabia and Yemen.

Durell looked toward the mainland and saw an Ethiopian gunboat shelling the low, rocky hills. An American-made F105 fighter bomber wheeled sharply above an orange-ribboned blossom of smoke. The government was making a show of chasing the ELF into the wasteland. Durell knew the ways of such terrorist bands: they were dispersed over the countryside by now, herding their sheep or cutting their grain.

Beyond the gunboat, the red tile roof of the beach club still smoldered, its concrete walls intact. The half-dozen small private airplanes that had been parked beside its landing strip when Durell flew in that morning were gone, except for one. It was a charred heap of twisted metal. Durell's charter pilot had left before the attack with instructions to return in two hours. It was long past that time now. Soldiers idled about the grounds of the club. Durell conjectured that they had been left to guard against looting. A helicopter fluttered up from the lawn, bearing the last of the dead and wounded northwest, toward Asmara.

That would be Durell's next destination.

He was glad he was not one of those being taken in the helicopter.

Pearl divers continued to work between the island and the mainland, unconcerned with the racket of the gunboat's sporadic barrage. Gulls scavenged around the boats, flying up in a white whirlwind as each round was fired, then settling back onto the water.

As Durell watched, a small workboat churned around the water. It groped its way back and forth among the pearl divers at slow speed, dragging the bottom. When it got too close, a Tigrinyan shouted curses at it for disturbing the oyster beds.

There was no sign of Sheba—if that was the real identity of the girl with the chocolate hair. Durell had taken care to cover himself in the stone doorway. He had drawn no fire, but she might not have seen him. He would have to wait until night to cross the open water.

He went back inside the *tukul*, his mind full of dark thoughts about Sheba and his mission.

"*Anchi!* You, girl!" Deste commanded.

The woman working over the cooking fire brought Durell a wooden bowl containing spicy *wat* with chunks of fish. She handed him a round, spongy cake of bread called *injera*.

Durell sampled the dish. It was laced with red pepper, but good. He ate with relish, spitting out the fish bones. Deste sat on the earthern floor in front of him, her knees nearly touching his. She watched him curiously.

Durell saw nothing sinister in her eyes. She would be too clever to let it show. He had no reason to believe or disbelieve what she had told him. You went by patterns, and the pattern for Deste had not been formed yet. That made her potentially very dangerous. She had pulled him from the water, but he had been saved from death before for ulterior purposes.

He hoped he would not have to kill Deste.

He hoped she would not try to kill him.

Suspicion was a perpetual traveling companion for Durell. He had learned early in life to look behind the faces others presented to the world. You usually found something quite different there, whether that face belonged to a woman, a man or a government. K Section had fully developed his instincts, making him into what he knew he was best suited to be—a solitary soldier, venturing amid the midnight armies of a planet that sometimes appeared bent on insanity and destruction.

He preferred the solo role in which his name never was mentioned in the applause. Danger and caution ran in his veins. He had learned to give and to take in the cities and jungles of the world. He was good at it.

Suddenly, Deste said, "Tell me about yourself." She had made up her mind about something, Durell thought.

"You know enough."

She hesitated, then placed her hand in his. Her delicate sand-colored fingers were lost in his loose grip. "It doesn't matter," she said. "You owe me a favor,"

"I thought so," Durell replied.

"You must help me get to Asmara."

The pieces of a puzzle all fell into place in Durell's mind. She could serve a purpose in a plan that he had been shaping.

"Tell me why," he said.

"I can't go alone. I have no means. I am a woman."

"It has to be more than that."

"All right." She took a deep breath and her proud breasts lifted the front of her *shamma*. "My mother was a member of an ancient noble family. My grandfather was a favorite at court, but long ago there was a political dispute. He was exiled to an *amba*, a high, flat-topped mountain. Emperors have always used the *ambas* to isolate pretenders to their thrones and nobles who were dangerous to them. My family never recovered the confidence of the court, but it was allowed to retain its titles and estates. Now the new government is suspicious of all of the *makuannent*, regardless of differences among them in the past. Many have been imprisoned; some have been executed. I am afraid I will share their fate if I am caught."

"So you are in hiding," Durell said.

"Exactly. I was doing research on the coast when the coup took place. I had been out of touch for weeks when I finally heard of it. I feared for my life. I didn't know

21

what to do, so I came here. I had worked among these people before. They gave me shelter. I had no money, but I promised I would pay them well. They are becoming impatient. They have gone through my suitcase and taken the only silk dress I packed. They also took my camera, although they don't know what to do with it. I must leave here. If you will take me to Asmara, I can find out how my family has fared."

"And if they have been taken into custody?"

"That is not your worry."

"Just keep that in mind," Durell said.

The gunboat slammed two more rounds into the air and the gulls squawked angrily. Durell wondered about what lay ahead of him as he waited in the smoky hut, smelling of fish and sweat. His enemies, shadowy, phantomlike, were out there. If they thought him dead now, they would recognize their mistake soon enough. And they were engaged in something so monstrous that they would go to any end to conceal it, until the right moment.

Then it would be too late to avoid awesome damage and horrible loss of life—without paying the price. And paying it again and again.

Durell recalled the photograph. It covered thousands of square miles. An intelligence analysis specialist had detected, almost lost in those vast distances, one tiny, brilliant pinpoint of light. Its source was unknown to any government.

He wondered: if maniacs could get what they asked by threatening an airliner with a hand grenade, how fantastic would be their demands through atomic blackmail?

4

The messages kept coming through the predawn darkness. They came from London, Buenos Aires, Capetown, Calcutta and Baghdad, as each man in his distant corner of the planet scrutinized his inner self and arrived at his personal commitment to help Durell if he could—and, if he could not, to avenge him.

Nothing like it had ever happened before.

The communications center in K Section's Washington headquarters hand-delivered each message to the desk of General McFee, who was now dressed in a gray pinstripe suit, white shirt and solid charcoal tie.

He felt ambivalent as he shuffled the forms.

He should be angry.

He had not authorized dissemination of a death report on Durell. Yet the requests had begun arriving only minutes after McFee himself had first been informed. In hindsight, he realized the impossibility of keeping the news from the men in the ranks. Agents frequently died in the performance of their duties. The dark gleaning and milling of information went on. But it was different with Cajun. Known only in legend to many of his colleagues, he had been their model, the paragon of their profession.

Contrary to McFee's fears about damaged morale, the response to the loss of Durell revealed a strength of heart and will to go forward that surprised the little gray man. So, although he should have been angry about the flaunting of broken security indicated by the messages, McFee instead allowed himself the semblance of a smile.

Sheba had communicated the subsequent reports McFee had demanded. She claimed to have seen Durell go under, either drowning or already dead. McFee ordered that she be queried again. He wanted every detail: how did she know the victim was Durell? How did she explain her escape, while Samuel, with all of his experience, had been killed?

McFee just could not believe that Durell was dead.

Sheba would have to prove it.

Yet, she was only an auxiliary; how much could he expect of her? Compared to the scope of K Section's responsibilities, its professionals were so few that locals and foreign-employed Americans had to be recruited to fill the gaps. Their duties were important, but normally routine. They read and listened, developed sources and gathered information. Once or twice a month, they forwarded the data to K Section for analysis. But sometimes they became pivotal to a mission; the professionals had to rely on them in the field.

They seldom liked the dangerous role.

Occasionally they brought disaster to an operation.

McFee studied the message of Tom Hennessey. He had radioed from Cairo, where he was running K Section's control temporarily.

Tom was built like a heavyweight boxer. He had the raw and ready manner of a honky-tonk bouncer—which he had been while earning his law degree from Duke University. He had a paranoiac streak that sometimes made him cruel and violent, but he got results, McFee reflected. He had worked in all quarters of the world. Now he was a scarred veteran in the prime of his career. He also was the closest K Section agent to Asmara, if you did not count Duncan Edmondson or Shep Calder. And they could not be spared from their posts in the Arabian oil sheikdoms.

In small, precise letters, McFee wrote "affirmative" in the line marked "Reply" at the bottom of Tom's printed message form. He initialed the form, then pressed a call button on his desk.

Tom was the man to get the whole story from Sheba.

He would have to do that quickly and move ahead with Sam's mission.

5

"Let me row," Deste whispered.

"Quiet!"

Durell's shoulder ached, but not badly. He leaned into each stroke of the oars deliberately, careful not to start the bleeding again. It was slow going. The boat moved soundlessly. He peered across the moon-beaded water toward the beach club, wondering where the soldiers were. He had lost sight of them, but he knew they were still

24

there. He had been watching for hours.

Deste knelt with her back to him, her knees in three inches of bilgewater that swept gently back and forth with the motion of the boat. The hood of her *shamma* covered her golden hair and spread a fan of shadow across her face. Durell sweated under one of the garments also.

The dinghy had seemed suspended between the island and mainland for hours.

Then it scrunched into the beach in the shade cast by the club's boat pier. A gentle surf sucked on the sand as Durell pulled the boat securely out of the water. The waves made purling noises among the pilings. Durell lifted Deste over the side of the boat. He was surprised at the feel of her. Her bones were small, but her muscles were hard just beneath her soft, womanly skin, harder than those of many men. He let her down inches from his face. Her eyes were calm, their irises the color of pewter. They told him he could depend on her.

He hoped they were not lying.

The sea soaked their flimsy cotton robes, plastering them to their calves. The wet cloth rustled as they darted across the beach in a low crouch. They looked like ghosts and sounded as if they were running on thin straw. In a landscape of black, gray and white, the *shammas* provided excellent camouflage, blending into the night shades of spiky desert growth.

Durell stopped in the shadow of a fig tree. "You know what to do?" he whispered. He did not take his eyes from the hulk of the club building.

"I am to go to the parking lot."

"Cars are still there. Find one with keys in the ignition. Be ready when I arrive." He scanned the building and grounds. The stark moonlight had tumbled the scene into eerie geometric shapes. "Go. Now!"

He watched for the soldiers as a moment passed and no sound came from Deste. He turned impatiently to urge her on: "I said . . ."

She was gone.

He caught a glimpse of her as she disappeared among boulders and scrub twenty yards up the slope. His ears had told him nothing. *Where had she learned to move like that?*

Durell crept toward the club's rear entrance. Training at the Farm maintained by K Section near Washington had sensitized his memory. The most casual perceptions were stored there for immediate recall. He knew the route he had taken that morning from the front entrance to the locker room, through the kitchen and out the rear exit, as well as if he had traversed it a thousand times.

The glow of a cigarette tugged his gaze to the left. A soldier idled away the hours squatting in a slab of black shadow near a corner of the building. His rifle leaned on the wall beside him.

Durell did not want to hurt him. He could kill in a dozen ways, with a finger, a hand, the heel of his foot. But he did so only when necessary. He flattened himself against the wall and inched toward the corner on silent, leather-thonged sandals.

The soldier hummed a tune in a sleepy, bored way.

All he felt was a firm pressure on his neck.

Durell fanned him for flashlight or matches. Hyenas chuckled nearby. A garbage can crashed onto its side. A couple of soldiers out of sight to Durell discussed the beasts in Amharic. Durell was familiar with the tongue as that of the dominant Amhara tribe and the official language of the country.

He stole into the building. The matches were not necessary in the kitchen where vaporous moonbeams silvered the disarray of pots and pans. A pool of blood told him the cooks had been unlucky. Lack of discrimination for the innocent was the most revolting characteristic of terrorists everywhere, Durell had found.

The hallway beyond was as black as the pupils of a corpse, but he needed no light there. He pushed open the door of the locker room. It smelled like a slaughterhouse. A cricket chirped. The concrete walls rang with the echo of water dripping from a shower head. Durell struck one of the soldier's matches with a thumbnail. He was standing in front of the locker he had rented. It was stippled with angry bullet holes. The match flame cast a yellow sheen onto a rind of blood covering the floor where the Italian

26

father and son had fallen. A thick smear led to where a hand had thrashed out.

Durell's locker was empty.

Looters must have got into the building in spite of the soldiers, he decided.

He briefly considered what to do. Then he pulled up the hem of his *shamma*. Working quickly, he unfastened the safety pin holding his key with its metal disc to his bathing suit. He straightened the pin into a long slender picklock and used it to open the other lockers.

Only his belongings appeared to have been taken. *Why?* It could not be merely because he had left his locker open. The lockers of the two Italians were open and their things were still in them.

He would miss the .38 S&W like an old and reliable friend. And the loss of his passport certainly could complicate matters.

The club catered to the wealthy. Almost any of the other lockers would have made a good night's work for an ordinary thief. Most of the wallets were stuffed with Ethiopian dollars and credit cards. Durell had supposed that the authorities would allow no one to tamper with the possessions; that they would demand supporting identification before releasing them to avoid claims and counterclaims later. But someone had got past them. Just long enough to empty Durell's locker. Again, he asked himself, "Why?"

Ignazio Bertollini.

Durell read the name on the Eritrean driver's permit, wondering if Ignazio were dead or alive. His physical description probably was as close to Durell's as he would find. Also in the ostrich-skin wallet were a club membership and other supporting identification, including a credit card of Eurocard International.

It would have been advantageous to Deste if he could have secured new identity papers for her as well, but he did not know the location of the women's lockers and dared not rummage through the building looking for them.

She would have to take her chances—just as she said she had been doing.

Durell heard the slap of footsteps in the hallway. He dropped the match and sprawled in the gore beside the row of lockers. He lay still, eyes shut, arms flung out.

He heard the footfalls pause at the door, then hurry to his side. He waited patiently, the cold smell of the dead men's blood strong in his nostrils. Then he felt the presence of the soldier bending over him. A finger poked his chest. "Corporal!"

At that instant, Durell opened his eyes. They stared straight into the young soldier's dark-skinned face. The man's jaw dropped in fright. Durell brought the edge of his palm in a hard overhead swing and popped him in the neck. He folded. He was not seriously injured, but the carefully calculated force of the blow had totally incapacitated him.

Durell jumped to his feet, almost tore an ankle ligament as he slipped on the blood, and ran toward the dining area and the front entrance to the building. A rifle fired three times, blindly; yells of alert, shouted commands came from behind.

He burst into the plush dining room, tripped over a fallen teak dining chair, hit the carpet, rolled and came up still running, fighting the entanglements of the *shamma*. Tatters of a half-burnt curtain ribboned the moonglow coming through a plate glass wall. Against the gleaming sea, beyond the curtains, forms gestured and moved in confusion. Flashlight beams diffused in bright clouds on the plate glass, spreading low light over the upset tables and broken dinnerware littering the floor. Durell was at the exit when the plate-glass window shivered, spitting chunks, then shattered inward in a storm of glittering daggers. The submachine gun bullets thumped into the walls around him with deadly urgency.

Then he was outside, in the parking lot. He ran past the first row of cars to the second, where he had told Deste to guide him with a flash of parking lights. The first row of automobiles would conceal the lights from anyone near the building.

Almost in front of him, the yellow parking lights blinked once.

He flung himself into the driver's seat of a little black

Fiat. Deste had the engine running. Durell glanced at her as they lurched from the parking slot, his foot heavy on the accelerator, the headlights off.

She looked back at the winks of rifle fire, then at Durell.

"You got it?" she asked.

He yanked the wheel and the steady little car swung with a squeal of tires onto the Asmara road. His lips were drawn back over his teeth as he gasped for breath. The loss of blood had weakened him more than he realized. "I got something," he said, nodding his head. He turned on the headlights.

"Very professional," she said. Her hands were clasped in her lap. She watched the road ahead as if on a Sunday drive. The glow from the instrument panel limned her aristocratic features against the darkness beyond. Durell looked hard at her. She was as cool as the moon that seemed to shine from her eyes.

He wondered where she had learned to use a word like "professional"—in a context like this.

6

"It's a roadblock."

"Are you certain?" Deste asked.

Durell braked the Fiat to a halt. After the rush of wind through its open windows, the silence was hard, crushing in on him. They were halfway up the wall of the great escarpment. Durell had been watching the headlights high above them for the last five minutes. There were two sets of them. They had not moved—until now.

As Durell considered what to do, they began descending, moving back and forth among trees and ridges along the twisting highway.

"They saw us stop; they're coming to find out why," he said.

"They could have seen us coming for half an hour from

up there. No one else is on the highway," Deste said. Her voice was flat, without panic.

Durell spun the steering wheel, thankful for the little car's short turning radius. He headed them back in the direction from which they had come. He would have preferred to turn the headlights off, but that was impossible. Some of the hairpin turns were banked against sheer drops of hundreds of feet and shaded from the light of the moon by massive cliffs.

"They must store maintenance supplies off of the road someplace," Durell said. "I saw a lane. . . ."

"That's the place," Deste said.

Durell turned into a stony trail where parallel tire tracks had beaten down the grass. If they got cornered here, there would be no driving out, he thought. The lane ascended onto a rectangular clearing where earthmovers had gouged out a hunk of the hillside and leveled the dirt and stone. A dense stand of bamboo walled most of the area, but it had been unable to get a foothold on the boulders torn from the face of the escarpment and pushed to the lip of the clearing. Those openings in the bamboo led to a thousand-foot drop and looked out onto the glowing night sky like doorways to eternity. A dense woods growing in a wet ravine loomed over the east side of the clearing. A waterfall splashed somewhere among the trees. Evidently the space served as a highway maintenance depot. Portable road barricades lay in a jumbled heap. Nearby was a steel drum containing gasoline, mounted with a hand pump. An eight-wheel dump truck sat beside a mound of crushed stone. It looked like one of those oversized jobs quarries used to make big deliveries. Its bed was piled high with a full load of gravel.

Durell parked close behind the huge truck where its tailgate bulked above his door. He heard the tortured transmission whine of heavy vehicles descending the highway in low gear. There was no time to spare.

"Roll up the windows and get out," he said.

"What are you going to do?" Deste asked as she whirled a window crank.

"We can't let them find the car." His door was so close

to the truck that he could not use it. He got out Deste's side of the Fiat, pushing her ahead of him.

Then he unfastened the truck's tailgate, found a flashlight in the cab and worked furiously under the hood to jump the ignition wiring. The clash of changing gears came from the highway as the vehicles pursuing him turned onto the trail and began their ascent toward the clearing.

Durell slammed the hood down and clambered into the cab, started the engine and threw the dump lever. The steel dump bed raised its massive load with implacable strength. The tons of gravel shifted suddenly with a shuddering, grinding roar and spilled over the Fiat. Durell hoped the little car was built strongly enough not to be crushed.

Quickly, he lowered the dump bed, killed the engine. He jumped from the truck and grabbed Deste's hand and ran for the junglelike woods. He could not see the headlights of the oncoming vehicles, but they cast a glow that lighted the sky just beyond the clearing. They would arrive any second.

Durell pressed through low brush and into the trees. The soggy forest floor was treacherous with fallen branches, protruding stones. He paused, Deste at his side. They were surrounded by the whine of insects, the peeping of tree frogs. A nightbird called mournfully.

A troop truck carrying a squad of soldiers parked in the middle of the clearing. Beside it was a Ferret armored scout car of British manufacture. A nasty looking 7.62 mm machine gun in its turret pointed skyward like the stinger of a scorpion.

Durell figured the unit had been stationed on the highway as a blocking force against the ELF after the raid on the Villa d'Este. It should have been withdrawn by now, but it was his bad luck that it had not been.

The vehicles kept their headlights on. A spotlight burned through the night from atop the Ferret. The soldiers spread across the clearing, rifles at the ready.

Durell and Deste slipped further into the woods.

A fallen branch popped under Deste's foot.

There was a command, then the mindless stutter of the 7.62, joined by the rattle of automatic rifle fire and lead, exploded from the clearing. Deste uttered a sharp little sound and dropped to the ground. Durell dived behind a rotten log. The firing lasted about fifteen seconds. Slugs thumped into trees and screamed wickedly off rocks. Leaves and twigs floated down through the steamy air. The echoes clamored angrily back and forth among the gorges that seamed the face of the escarpment.

When it was over, the natural sounds of night had stopped. Except for that of the waterfall. Durell was almost at its foot.

He could not see Deste. "Are you all right?"

There was no answer for a moment. Then she whispered, "I—I think so."

The Ferret grunted through the brush at the edge of the woods. It stopped with its steel bow bruising trees where the deep forest began. Its headlights glared among the trees and ferns and creepers. The hot grasp of its spotlight swept back and forth and the squad of soldiers moved cautiously down into the woods.

Durell kept Deste beside him and made his way around the line of troops until he was back at the outer edge of the clearing, behind the bamboo screen. He knelt beside an opening in the bamboo where a flat boulder overhung the precipice. He could sense the open air of the abyss, but it was so dark he could not see into it.

"Take off your *shamma*," he whispered.

"I have nothing on under it."

"Give it to me!"

Deste pulled the garment over her head and handed it to him. She clasped her arms over her small, exquisitely molded breasts. She shivered despite the heat of the night. Durell ripped the thin cloth down the middle, dividing it in half. He pried two large stones from the loose dirt and tied one into a corner of each half, leaving most of the material free.

"Now scream."

"But—they'll hear . . ."

"Scream as loud as you can, just once."

Deste's eyes told Durell she thought the hours of strain had shattered his mind. She hesitated. He caught her arm and shook her. "There's no time to explain. Scream!"

This time she did not hesitate. She screamed with all of her might, as if at fate, savoring the release, gouging the soft air with her shrill ululation. Durell's ears rang. He heard the soldiers call to each other. They were coming out of the woods on the double.

"Get back into the trees, the way we came," he said.

Deste ran away behind the bamboo screen, crouching low, daggers of moonshine turning to silvery oil on her skin. Durell waited until he heard the crunch of running boots only a few feet away. Then he tossed the weighted cloths over the verge and scrambled into the shadows. He heard the clatter of tumbling stones far below.

"Bring the searchlight!" an officer ordered.

Durell watched the light dance across the clearing in the hands of a running soldier. He looked down as its beam picked out the white triangles of cloth.

No one spoke for a moment.

"There could be others," someone said.

"We shall see. Fan out. Search the woods."

Durell beat the party back to the rotten log and took Deste into a hollow behind the falls. He had figured a cavity would be there, hewn from the stone by tons of water during countless rainy seasons. When the rains fell, the swollen stream would hammer lethally down the twenty-foot drop. Now it spread lazily in a skirt of glass.

The fragmented gleam of light from the vehicles wavered in the green skin of falling water; its glow barely penetrated into the cave. Durell and Deste sat against the wall, getting their breath.

"What if they find us? We have no place to run."

"They won't find us."

Durell took off his *shamma* and bent over a pool just inside the falls.

"What are you doing?" Deste asked.

"I can't go into Asmara with blood all over this thing. Now's a good chance to wash it." He rubbed the soggy garment against the stone floor.

"You're all business," Deste said.

"You've got to take the opportunities as they come." He felt her crawl next to him. He did not look around. "It's all I've got to wear, besides my bathing suit," he said.

"That's more than I have. It's cold in here."

"You've got clothes in your bag."

"If they don't find the car," she said. She knelt against his back and looked over his shoulder. The soft orb of her breast was pillowed against his shoulder blade. He was aware of its small nipple pressing into his flesh. The muscles in his stomach and loins gripped pleasantly.

Her lips brushed his ear. "Your skin is hot," she whispered.

7

A midmorning sun stabbed at the falls and the splashing water made a sound like hot grease in a frying pan. The humidity was suffocating when Durell awoke. He looked at Deste. She was curled on her side, her small hands pillowing her cheek, her ripe, chiseled lips slightly parted.

Durell touched her. She looked at him through big eyes confused with sleep. Then she remembered and she smiled.

He went to the clearing, found a rusty shovel and dug the Fiat out of the gravel pile. Sweat soaked the back of his *shamma* and fine grit covered his face by the time he was through, but he was thankful to find that the car was only scratched and dusty.

He took Deste's bag to her and they bathed in the pool behind the falls. Then he returned to the relative coolness of the windswept clearing to wait for her to dress. The area was littered with spent cartridges. As he had expected, the military's search had been apathetic after the ruse. They probably had decided the car they followed had dropped off a couple of suspects here, then somehow evaded them and escaped in the direction of Massawa. They had been satisfied with the discovery of the two "bodies" at the foot of the cliff and had pulled out of the area shortly afterward.

Durell stood at the edge of the clearing and looked across the lowlands toward the Red Sea. Below him a bearded vulture soared along the basaltic face of the massif, looking for bones to drop and break for their marrow. Colobus monkeys chattered in the forest, feeding among its orchids. Durell heard the call of red-winged touracos.

Then Deste was beside him, dressed in skirt, blouse and low-heeled slippers, and it took Durell a moment to become accustomed to her that way. She had brushed her hair. The sun shone in its golden waves. The way he had seen her the day before in the homespun cotton robe and dirty stone hut seemed unreal.

"It's beautiful, isn't it?" she said as the warm updraft played in her hair.

"Yes." Durell was thinking how few moments he had to spare for beauty. No matter where he was, the world for him was sinister, shadowed in constant danger, stark with urgency. "Let's move," he said as he turned toward the Fiat. "It's still sixty kilometers to Asmara."

The ELF emergency apparently had expired. The roadblock had been lifted, as Durell had expected it would be by morning. Traffic was heavy now and he had to watch out for trucks hurtling toward Massawa. As the highway continued to zigzag upwards in hairpin turns they sometimes crossed fine stone bridges still bearing the symbol of the Italian Fascists who had built them. The Fascists had killed countless Ethiopians, many of them as forced laborers pressed into building these marvelous roads. Despite the grisly toll, the emperor had declared that there should be no vengeance taken against the Italians when he regained his domain. Too many men in high places had collaborated with them.

Durell found Asmara, Ethiopia's second largest city, perched on the brink of the Rift Valley at 7,500 feet. The tropical sun sparkled on its buildings. The thin, crisp air reminded Durell of Mexico City.

Deste directed him toward the home of a man she called *Dejasmatch* Nadu Ambaw, saying he had ties throughout the highlands, and that she could trust him. Durell remembered that *Dejasmatch*—Leader of the Outside—was a title conferred in the old days on officers who camped around the emperor's tent as an inner guard. It marked Ambaw as a nobleman of important stature.

The Italians had built Asmara on the site of a village as the capital of their Eritrean colony. Its wide streets were thick with cars and trucks, public buses, and little two-wheeled carriages called gharries. A breeze rippled the umbrellas of countless sidewalk cafes and bent the fronds of palm trees lining the avenues.

It looked to Durell as if the town had been brought stone by stone from Italy. As if in return, the Fascists had looted ancient artifacts of gem-encrusted gold wherever they had found them. And Mussolini had stolen the great obelisk from Aksum, the Queen of Sheba's capital in the time of Solomon. He had shipped its massive granite blocks to Rome and put them together again at the entrance to the Baths of Caracalla in the Piazza del Circo Massimo.

Durell drove around the base of a hill crowned by a Coptic church and, about two miles further, entered a shallow, gardenlike valley studded with eucalyptus trees. Its slopes were checkered with the homes of the wealthy.

"What kind of man is Ambaw?" he asked.

"I've never met him," Deste said.

Durell glanced at her. She watched the passing sights as if on tour. "How do you know what you are getting us into?" he asked.

She smiled and placed a small, golden hand on his knee. "Don't you think you can trust me—after last night, dear Sam?"

"No. Especially not after last night."

She laughed, as if to herself, and snuggled closer to him. A moment later she straightened and said, "Turn in here."

A high stone wall concealed Ambaw's Italian-style villa. A gatekeeper dressed in khaki shorts and shirt with epaulets listened as Deste spoke in Amharic. He answered in servile tones, but the eyes of a watchdog peered from the furrows of his aged face. He phoned from the gatehouse, came back and told them to park inside the compound. Two guards holding old Mauser rifles in their long skinny arms slouched against the wall of the veranda. A servant met Durell and Deste at the steps and showed them inside.

One of the guards followed them into a cool room with a high ceiling and an ivory and blue Kashan rug on the floor, then into a library. Above the bookcases encircling the room, the walls were mounted with antique weapons and photographs of fierce-looking men in rigid poses with their rifles. In a grouping near a fireplace were a sofa, wing chairs and desk. The desk held a sectioned agate paperweight the size of half a grapefruit and bookends made from the horns of walia ibex.

Ambaw was waiting there. He was short and fleshy. The coat of his white linen suit was a bit too small for his muscular shoulders. His eyes were dark, secretive slots. They revealed nothing but suspicion as his glance flickered over them. His hammerlike chin exuded authority.

He looked to Durell like a man accustomed to living and commanding by simple, strict codes.

"Greetings, *Dejasmatch* Ambaw," Deste said. "I bring you a spy."

Durell's first instinct was to run, but the guard stood in the doorway. He could take the guard, but not without alerting the whole compound. There were other armed men, then the wall, all in broad daylight. He told himself to relax; he might as well find out what he was to be hung for.

He saw that Ambaw was as surprised as he. Ambaw blinked, tapped the ashes of his Turkish cigarette into an alabaster ash tray. "A spy, you say?"

Deste nodded eagerly.

"And who are you, my dear?" Ambaw coaxed in a gravelly voice.

"Deste Giroud, *Dejasmatch* Ambaw. We have mutual friends in the movement." Her chin was thrust out proudly, like a soldier's.

"Ah! Yes, your name has reached me." Ambaw turned to Durell. He frowned. His voice became threatening. "If you are a spy, who pays you?"

"Ask her. I'm as curious as you," Durell said.

"He is an American spy," Deste said. "He was to meet Mira Seragate at the usual place, the island. But she tried to kill him. I was there. I saw it. It could only be because he was sent to thwart us."

"Is it true?" Ambaw asked.

"A girl shot at me," Durell said.

"She missed, but he had been wounded by the ELF," Deste said.

"I heard about the raid," Ambaw said.

"I pulled him from the water," Deste said. "He was half out of his mind. He rambled in his dreams. He mentioned Mira's code name, Sheba."

At least that cleared up the lingering question in Durell's mind about whether the girl who had shot at him was really Sheba. But it raised a lot of questions about Deste; about why Sheba had tried to kill him; about what plot he was supposed to be thwarting.

"So you know Mira's American code name," Ambaw said.

"I don't know anything," Durell replied. "I tried to help Deste out and this is what I get. I'm going to walk out of here and forget this happened—unless you try to stop me." He moved toward the door. The guard did not get out of his way. When they were a foot apart, the guard swung the butt of his rifle at Durell's midsection, but Durell sidestepped, caught the heavy weapon with a twisting motion and, using the guard's own momentum, slammed the stock against the guard's jaw, dropping him. The guard had strong hands. He was in a daze, but he clung to the rifle. Durell started to run past him. He thought he could surprise the other guard on the veranda. The struggle had been brief and silent.

"Stop!"

Durell looked back over his shoulder. It was Ambaw. He held a German P-38 pistol. The hard set of his jaw and the eager look in his eyes said he would use it. It was an inaccurate piece, but it would be stupid to bank on that.

Durell came back into the room. The guard rubbed his jaw and got to his knees.

"You are a bit of a problem," Ambaw said. His voice was tight and angry.

He waved the gun at a chair. "Sit down. What is your mission? Will you help us restore the monarchy, or has your government reversed its position?"

"Don't you see?" Deste said. "He is against us. That can be the only reason Mira tried to kill him. She and Ineyu have stood by us; they believe in our cause."

Durell said nothing. He was not surprised to find a plot afoot to restore the monarchy. It always happened when a king was toppled, but it seldom succeeded.

"Then there will be no more funds for Ineyu to give us? Speak!" Ambaw demanded.

Durell tried to make sense of what he was hearing. He had no knowledge of U.S. assistance for an uprising against the new military government. If such existed, he should have been informed. Either someone in K Section had screwed up by not telling him—and that was unlikely—or he had stumbled onto a deception of unknown proportions by Ineyu.

One thing was certain: he could offer Ambaw no help and that would be interpreted as opposition.

"Look," Durell said, "until a month ago, I thought Eritrea was somewhere in the West Indies. Then I saw this travel agent in Indianapolis. He said, 'You want to go somewhere different?' So here I am. I thought a swim in the Red Sea would be something, but this has it topped. I'm a tourist."

"A tourist!" Deste spat out the word. "You should have seen him last night. If he were a tourist, he would be dead."

"You should have seen her last night." Durell smiled.

The pistol hung loosely in Ambaw's hand. The guard had resumed his position, but now he had the barrel of the rifle pointed at Durell and his finger on the trigger. Durell saw the lust for his blood in the guard's eyes. The atmosphere had become decidedly ominous.

"You don't expect me to believe you," Ambaw said.

"Not really," Durell replied.

"Perhaps you do not realize the difficulties of my situation. I am under police surveillance. Tonight I leave for the mountains and nothing must interfere with my plans."

"Take me with you, *Dejasmatch* Ambaw," Deste cried. "Please. I'll die for the revolution." Her face was twisted with emotion. Her eyes gleamed like the silver inlay on the Arabian muskets on the wall behind her.

Durell decided she was overplaying her role, but he saw that Ambaw was impressed.

"You do not know what you ask, my dear. Life is difficult in the mountains. Besides, the people are fearful and suspicious. They are passing insane tales of a devil's light and a *zar*, a spirit who brings sickness, loosed from the doors of Satan himself. A stranger would be in great danger among them."

Durell sat up, wanting to hear more, but Deste intervened.

"I'll face any danger," she said.

Ambaw put a fatherly hand on her shoulder. "We shall see," he said. "The first hurdle is the ELF. It strikes the Asmara to Gondar highway almost daily. It has kidnapped many people. Not all of them have returned alive. Some of them were Americans." He looked at Durell. "Your agency will be most distressed when the ELF gets a second chance at you tonight—and succeeds."

"So you have alliance with the ELF as well as the monarchists," Durell said. "Doing an act like that can be dangerous."

Ambaw laughed. His teeth looked like yellow stones. "I have no alliance with those devils, my friend. But when you are shot to death and left in a burning car, the ELF will be blamed."

His face became stony. "By now, you see, it does not matter who you are. You have heard too much," he said grimly.

He opened a liquor cabinet. "Do you drink?"

"I like bourbon and soda."

Ambaw placed a decanter of whiskey and a seltzer bottle on his desk. "Make yourself comfortable. Drink as much as you like. You have until nightfall."

He went out the door with Deste and she gave him a backward glance he could not fathom. The midnight moons of her irises revealed triumph and sorrow, elation and dread; a thousand things.

Durell's blue eyes went almost black as he returned her glance.

Ambaw left the guard posted outside the locked door. Durell sat in a comfortable wing chair, sipping bourbon and soda. When ten minutes had passed, he unfastened the latched window and raised it easily. He could get out of the house, but there still was the armed guard on the veranda. He would have to pass him to escape the walled compound.

Durell regarded the room for a long moment. The only way to break out was with a gun, but the antique firearms cluttering the wall were useless. He must take the rifle from the guard at the library door. To do that, he had to lure him within striking distance and surprise him before he could pull the trigger—and there would be no margin for error. A bullet from the powerful Mauser would disable Durell no matter where it hit him.

At least he had plenty of time to prepare.

He rummaged through Ambaw's desk until he found a box of matches. Then he used books to start a fire in the fireplace. He took a cushion from the couch, ripped the fabric to expose wads of cotton stuffing and laid it on the fire, torn side down. In a few moments the cotton blazed and bright coals burrowed deep into its simmering depths, producing enormous quantities of thick, gray smoke. Durell opened the damper all the way so that most of the smoke went out the chimney. He did not want to alert the guard prematurely.

When he was ready he closed the window and the damper and carried the smoldering cushion across the room and held it close to the door. Smoke hazed the room now and his eyes watered and his throat stung with every breath as the draft sucked its tendrils through the crack beside the door.

The lock clicked almost immediately; the knob turned. Durell moved back a step and waited, every muscle tensed. This was the guard he had just humiliated in front of Ambaw, and Durell recalled the fierce pride of Ethiopians that stemmed from the not distant time when almost to

41

a man they considered themselves warriors in the fullest sense of the word. The man doubtlessly hated him now and would shoot on the slightest pretext. Durell had to make every move count.

Then the guard shoved the door open with his hip, rifle ready in both hands. He had no chance to aim before Durell hurled the burning cushion into his face, muffling his cry of terror.

He dropped the rifle, gasped, staggered, brushed frantically at the bright, wriggling sparks that clung to him from eyes to chest. Before his singed lips could utter another sound, Durell rammed his knuckles into the man just below the breastbone with all the strength he could muster. The guard fell with an agonized gasp.

Durell dragged him inside the library, took the rifle and moved soundlessly toward the veranda door. Soon the stench of smoke would bring others, but for the moment the compound was filled with the casual sounds of an ordinary day. A pot banged in the kitchen; birds chirped in the shrubs; a truck throbbed past on the street beyond the wall.

He pushed open the veranda door and the guard turned, half-lifted his rifle to fire. Durell's Mauser barked and the bullet threw the man onto his back.

Durell leaped from the veranda, running for the Fiat. He had turned the car toward the street entrance before anyone appeared. He glanced at his rear-vision mirror as he careened down the driveway. In that instant, he saw Ambaw knock a man's rifle barrel into the air. There was no sound of a shot.

Ambaw had said he was under police surveillance—evidently he would not increase the risk of bringing the authorities down on him with more firing.

Durell loosened his grip on the wheel and let out a long, slow breath as he drove through the open gate and headed for his hotel.

8

The devil's light. Durell remembered the

satellite photo with its piercingly bright point of light, bright enough to have been caused by a release of primordial energy.

A spirit who brings sickness. Radiation sickness.

Durell's brush with Ambaw had paid off. His hands trembled slightly on the steering wheel. Ambaw's chance remarks had indirectly confirmed the worst fears of K Section. The day of atomic anarchy had dawned. Only the most sinister of motives—blackmail, terrorism, greed for power—could be attributed to the private acquisition of atomic weapons.

And this had to be a private effort.

K Section had forecast such an eventuality. It had been only a matter of time. The materials, enriched uranium or plutonium, would have been obtained illegally from some small country that had joined the bourgeoning "nuclear club" of nations with atomic reactors to generate electric power. There were over a score of such nations and the list was growing almost monthly.

The techniques of uranium enrichment and plutonium recycling from power plant wastes were becoming common currency. More and more tons of devilishly destructive material were floating around the world in various stages of transportation and refinement, with processing going on in numerous plants.

If it had not been for the coincidental overflight of the RT12, which had been programmed for geophysical research, the blast might have gone undetected. Even then, K Section might have attributed the curious photograph to a malfunction and shelved the matter, but there had been other circumstances. Analysis of spectrographic readings had strongly indicated an atomic explosion.

And it had been impossible to raise Ineyu Worota. The

radio waves had traveled halfway around the world, then dropped into a void of enigmatic silence. The embassy had been contacted. It could not account for Ineyu's disappearance.

The timing had led General McFee to theorize that it had something to do with the apparent nuclear detonation. And Durell had agreed.

Durell glanced into his rearview mirror. A green Volkswagen was only a couple of car lengths behind him. It had been tailing him since he drove out of Ambaw's gate. There were no markings on it, but it had to be the police. They had Ambaw staked out.

When he reached the heart of the city, Durell parked at a large open air market and waited. The smell of oranges, figs and fresh mutton wafted out of the stalls, mingling with that of donkey droppings. Heavy slabs of salt brought in from the Denakil depression lay in long rows on the ground. Crowds of shoppers in Western and native dress milled about. The square was surrounded by tin-roofed buildings.

An officer dressed in mufti came from the VW and asked Durell for his identification. Durell saw a .32 Beretta in a holster on his belt as he handed him Ignazio Bertollini's driver's license. Durell considered all of the things for which he could be arrested—and spend priceless time in jail. He was driving a stolen car. He was using stolen identification papers. He had consorted with Ambaw and might be suspected of plotting treason.

The officer leaned against the Fiat's window sill and looked closely at Durell. His mouth was set in a hard, straight line.

"You will get out of the car, please." It was polite, but it was an order.

Durell saw him place the heel of his hand on the butt of his pistol. A long brown figner unsnapped the holster's safety strap.

Durell started counting options. There were not many. "What's the matter, officer?" he asked in Italian.

"This car: it is not yours, *signore*."

"Of course not. It's rented." Durell had noticed the rental company's label glued to the dash. He was playing for time, an unguarded moment. Pedestrians were beginning to stop and watch.

"But you did not rent it. We have checked by radio. This car was rented yesterday morning here in Asmara. It was rented by a woman named Deste Giroud."

Of course, Durell thought. She had driven to Massawa the same morning he was to meet Sheba, apparently planning to learn as much as she could about that meeting, then report to the monarchists. But Durell had fallen into her hands. When she realized what a prize she had, she did not waste time going back to her lower-echelon friends. She had gone straight to the top—Ambaw. Such a bold move would have been designed to secure her prestige in the group. There was always infighting for influence in conspiracies where a strong chain of command did not exist, and it was worst among royalists where such authority as there was often stemmed from hereditary titles, rather than ability.

The cop was grinning, waiting for Durell to say something.

Suddenly Durell straightened his arms with all of his strength and shoved the car door into him, knocking him back several feet. He plunged from the car in the same motion and rammed the cop in the chest with his good shoulder. The officer gave a grunt and sprawled onto the street as Durell ran into the crowded market place.

"*Fermi!* Stop!" the cop yelled.

Durell ran for an alley.

He heard the little Beretta pop twice and knew by the texture of the sound that the policeman had fired into the air. He would not dare shoot into the throng.

Durell had taken a room at the Ras Hotel the previous day, after arriving by EAL jet via Cairo and Khartoum. It was one of those old but prosperous hotels, informal, slightly run down and comfortable. As with most things in Asmara, the Italians had built it. They had wanted to show the Ethiopians what a real hotel was like, so they had used tons of imported marble and lots of gilt. It had a huge, superbly equipped kitchen, where Italian cooks still turned out the best *bistecca alla Fiorentina* Durell had ever eaten. And it had the most undependable steam heating system he had ever encountered for an establishment of its pretensions. The closets were stuffed with blankets to use against the chill nights nearly a mile and a half above sea level.

The Ras was a few blocks from the railroad station, on a wide boulevard that split into a V where it came to a park containing the former colonial administration buildings. Durell came out of the back streets onto the boulevard a block from the hotel.

He followed a walk flanked by gardens, passed under a green, yellow and red Ethiopian flag, and entered the main lobby. He read the scene with one trained sweep of his eyes, from the pale rectangle where the late emperor's picture had been removed, to the mahogany reception desk with its carved coat of arms of the House of Savoy and *Vitt. E. III*, recalling another emperor who no longer reigned. The tourist business was off because of the ELF, but businessmen, diplomats and technicians from Norway, Japan, Russia, the U.S. and African countries gave the lobby a busy look.

Durell spotted the lookout immediately. He was black and beefy, dressed in a dark blue suit of summer weight material. His bloodshot eyes had probably read every word in the *Addis Zemen* a dozen times. He held the rumpled newspaper just below his broad nose. Durell recognized yesterday morning's headlines on it.

Durell strolled to the newsstand, thumbed through a magazine, glanced back at the man. For an instant, their eyes locked. Then both looked away.

There was a car-rental booth in a corner of the lobby. Durell went there and ordered a car under his own name and asked that it be added to his room bill. If the police checked the rental agencies they would never connect his name with the Ignazio Bertollini who had fled from them at the market.

Durell got his room key and entered a stairwell, climbed a few steps, then went back down to where he could see into the lobby again.

The lookout was in a telephone booth, talking rapidly and gesturing with the rolled newspaper.

Alarms began ringing in Durell's brain. He climbed to the third floor and cautiously nudged the door open. He could see down the hallway past his room. No one was waiting.

He examined the door to his room quickly but with care. A dark sliver of paper almost the same color as the door was exactly where he had left it an inch from the bottom of the door. But someone had handled it.

The chemical coating was sensitive to perspiration. The strip of paper showed pale thumbprint lines. The boys in K Section's basement laboratory were always coming up with a new gimmick. This one was pretty good, Durell thought.

He cautiously unlocked the door and pushed it open with his toe. The alarms became louder as the door swung silently on oiled hinges. Durell figured the lookout had called to alert a confederate waiting in the room—but it was empty.

He spent about fifteen minutes going through the IPS formula, securing the room. He had placed his suitcase the distance of his thumbnail from the back wall of his closet. Now it was a couple of inches from the wall. He opened it. Nothing appeared to have been taken. The small Mk6 transceiver was still there. He switched on its power.

K Section would be awaiting his report.

An SR71 was to have flown over the Simien Mountains the previous afternoon; by now an analysis of its high altitude photographs should be ready with map coordinates of the blast site. Durell would ask for that. Then it would be up to him to go to the scene—and find out who was responsible.

Durell also hoped that McFee would authorize some kind of approach to the local authorities so as to take the heat off him. Being a fugitive was not making his mission any simpler.

The call would go to Cairo and be relayed from there through London. Cairo was Tom Hennessey, code name Dukes. Durell began to transmit.

"Dukes from Cajun. Dukes from Cajun. Come in, Dukes."

Silence.

Durell remembered the lookout, the telephone call. He took a chair from the desk beside his bed and propped it under the knob of his door. He came back and tried to call Hennessey again. Still no luck.

Cairo was a twenty-four-hour relay. Someone was supposed to man it day and night.

Durell showered and shaved. He was hungry, but he did not want to take the time to eat. He put a fresh bandage on the shoulder wound and dressed in a gray suit, white shirt and blue knit tie.

Then he sat on the edge of the bed and tried the radio again. "Dukes, Dukes from Cajun. Come in."

Again there was no reply.

Durell turned the transmitter over and unsnapped the back cover. He swore softly. The tuning coil was missing. If he had been willing to believe the fault lay at the other end of the call, he could have gone for hours, even days, without finding out.

He stared at the useless piece of electronic gear. His only link with K Section was Sheba's transmitter, and that was awkward. Sheba had tried to kill him. Maybe she had stolen the coil, just in case he had survived. It could not have been done by Ambaw and his gang; they had not known of his presence.

But there could be a third party. Someone not necessarily associated with either Sheba or Ambaw. Someone who had the maniacal audacity to tamper with the world's shaky atomic equilibrium.

The alarms jangled louder as Durell considered that possibility.

He slightly parted the jute curtains of his window and scanned the boulevard and hotel drive. There were loiterers among the strollers and trinket vendors, but he could not be sure that any of them was watching his room.

The telephone rang. It was a clerk telling him the rental car he had ordered, a tan BMW, waited outside the hotel entrance.

The time had come to find out about Sheba. She lived near the stadium, not far from the Eritrean quarter, on the north side of the city.

Durell saw that the lookout was gone when he passed

48

through the lobby. He had probably been replaced by another. The bar, with its mounted leopard and lion heads, was alive with the murmur of an afternoon crowd. A couple of Russians in nearly identical open-neck sports shirts were smoking and drinking vodka. Durell pegged them for technicians from a listening base the Russians had built near America's Kagnew communication facilities just outside of town. The ELF was constantly harrassing Kagnew, but always seemed to leave the Russians alone, he reflected. Afars on a buying mission from Djibouti sipped anisette and discussed the market in French.

Durell sensed that something was wrong the moment he stepped into the sunlight.

He went to the car and hesitated with his hand on its door, then opened the hood and checked to make sure the ignition had not been wired to a bomb. It was clean, but he still did not feel right as he drove onto the boulevard.

He had gone only a couple of blocks when the steering went mushy. He parked beside the curb and inspected the tires. Air was hissing from the one on the left front. It was going down fast and was almost flat. He took off his coat, dreading the hot work of changing it.

Then he realized the air was coming out of the valve stem. He looked closely. The valve core had been unscrewed.

The alarms started screaming.

Durell took one of Ignazio's plastic-coated credit cards and laid it on the trunk lid. He unlocked the trunk but held the lid so that it rose just enough to insert the edge of the card into the opening. He slid the card from the corner of the trunk toward the center.

It struck something after going about six inches.

It was the plunger of a negative pressure detonator.

Durell's throat went tight. He thought what would have happened if he had opened the trunk to look for a bomb as he had done with the hood.

They had been clever. And they had worked fast, indicating good organization. The lookout had earned his pay—he had seen Durell make the rental arrangements and relayed the word. Then they would have bribed the rental clerk for the number of the car and the garage attendant to look the other way while they fixed it.

Durell had no pocket knife. It had been stolen with his slacks. But he still carried the locker key with its metal disc. It was the only tangible piece of identification he would have when he confronted Sheba. He inserted the disc into the thin slot and held the plunger of the detonator down with it. Then he let the trunk lid rise.

A half-pound of JP plastic explosive lay just inside the trunk well next to the latch assembly. It was enough to blow the car to bits and Durell with it.

He yanked the fuse out of the soft cube.

It was harmless now.

He wiped the sweat from his face. His hand felt cold. Then he changed the tire and headed for Sheba. She might be just as deadly as the stuff riding behind him, he thought. And who knew what would come after her?

His job had hardly begun.

9

Gold letters on the display window said:
MIRA

Abiti Per Signora

It was a dress shop—Sheba's cover.

Durell parked his BMW nearby. A gabble of voices, Ethiopian, Arabian, European, replaced the sound of the car's motor as he regarded the scene from beneath a lowered sun visor.

Clots of strollers coursed past the juniperlike zeba trees in patined bronze kettles flanking the shop entrance. Shoppers and street vendors overflowed into the cobblestone thoroughfare where they dodged gharries and donkeys, autos and a lurching General Ethiopian Transport Company bus. Ragged boys carrying wooden trays of goods, called for buyers of chewing gum, socks, skins of colobus monkeys and condoms.

Durell decided the confusion made it impossible to tell if the shop were under surveillance.

This had once been a prime neighborhood, he thought. Now rotting wooden eaves and peeling paint blemished the row of two-story, yellow-stone structures containing the dress shop, but most of the stores still looked moderately prosperous. A branch of the Banco di Roma was only a few doors away.

As Durell watched, a big man a couple of inches taller than himself came out of Mira's. Durell instantly recognized him as Tom Hennessey, the "Dukes" whose Cairo Control he had attempted to radio from the Ras Hotel. Hennessey brushed past a devout Amhara who had just stopped a turbaned priest to kiss his silver cross. Huge hands hung from the cuffs of his blue suit. His head was a rugged block of pink capped with a kinky, silver floss. Restrained havoc glinted from his sky-blue eyes as he paused, looked unhurriedly right and left. Satisfied, he moved through the crowd with the menace of an avalanche. He got into a white Volvo and it disappeared around the first corner on mewing tires.

Durell waited and studied the dress shop, aware of the scent of burning eucalyptus logs used by Ethiopians as fuel. The sky was an empty blue shell, yellow around the edges. The afternoon sun shattered on the display window. He could not see inside.

There would be an apartment above the store, maybe a rooftop exit. You could go from one roof to the next without difficulty, he decided.

He considered the meaning of Hennessey's presence. He could have confronted him, but his instinct told him to hang back, wait and see. His methodical mind categorized the North Carolinian's appearance at this particular time and place. Either it was authorized, or it was not. The latter possibility was real, if remote, and it made Durell cautious.

He had worked with Hennessey once, briefly. It had been a routine assignment in Brazil—if there were such a thing as a routine assignment in this business. There had been a rebellion by noncommissioned officers of the Brazilian army, and he and Hennessey had assisted authorities in tracking the cause to the notorious Dmitri Alekseevich Diakanov, a senior KGB officer in the country as a member of a Soviet "Peace Prize Commission." Hennessey, an ex-Navy SEAL recruited by K Section early in the Vietnam conflict, had shown a disagreeable fondness for violence. Just winning was not enough for him. He wanted to win big—and that had led to excesses, Durell recalled.

Once he had crushed a disarmed man's gunhand in his fist as if he were cracking a couple of walnuts.

He would try to make points after the game was over. It went with his cunning. He took few risks.

Durell approached the shop with care. Uncle Sam was a silent partner in its operation, which was supposed to turn a profit. But when Mira Seragate—who was Sheba—found business going sour, she could count on a few American dollars to carry her through the slump. The money came in an ordinary white envelope, along with a slightly ungrammatical letter from an Uncle Joseph that told of weather and relatives in New York City.

Anyone with enough curiosity to check would find that Mira did have an Uncle Joseph in New York. But it was next to impossible to unsnarl the chain by which K Section funneled the money to him.

Business often was bad for Sheba.

The currency came frequently, wrinkled old bills that looked as though they had been stuffed in a sock.

Durell glanced through the door window. The girl with the chocolate hair was more beautiful than he had remembered. A healthy luster shone on her skin. A candle-fire glow lighted the dark, almond eyes above her high cheekbones. There was nothing mysterious about her pouting lips or her long, supple legs. She wore a skirt of russet plaid and a single bow at her narrow waist held a wraparound maroon top of clinging, revealing knit.

She was preoccupied as he had expected, taking payment for a confection of lace and silk from the fashionably bony wife of a Canadian diplomat—Durell had seen the red and white fender flags on a Lincoln parked in front of the store.

Durell entered, turned quickly away and waited. He wanted her within reach and the shop empty when she realized who he was.

His permanent Q clearance freed him to do his job however he deemed necessary, but he regarded it as unfortunate that circumstances had forced him to come here. A cardinal rule of the business was that you took no unnecessary chances with your assignment—even your life was secondary to that. If he blew Sheba's cover now, it could endanger his mission. But her transmitter was his only remaining link with K Section and all of its powerful resources. Moreover, he still lacked the intelligence she was to have given him at the Villa d'Este.

And there were all sorts of nagging questions about why she had tried to kill him.

The smell of new fabric hung in the warm, still air. Racks of dresses filled every nook of the store. Durell pretended to inspect them as he recalled Sheba's dossier in photographic detail.

KAPPA SIGMA 7F/2901 Rating AA
SUBJECT: SERAGATE, Mira Sophia
MARITAL STATUS: Single
AGE: 26
ORIGINS: Born Biskia, Eritrea Prov., Ethiopia. Parents, banana growers, now deceased. Paternal and maternal grandparents emigrated Naples, Italy to Eritrea, all deceased. No other immediate relatives.
EDUCATION: High School Equivalent. OJT secretarial, AFI, Kagnew Communications Facility, Asmara, Ethiopia.
MALE FRIENDS: Numerous (see File KAPPA SIGMA 7F/2901b).
FEMALE FRIENDS: Unknown
MISCELLANEOUS: Associated with K Section through Jerome Acton of State and John D. Dawson, Maj. USAFI.
MULTILINGUAL: Italian, English, Amharic, Tigrynian; some proficiency Arabic, Russian.
COMMENT: Subject reared on small holding granted parents by Eritrean Colonial Administration of Italian Empire. Subsistence level minimum. When not assisting on family tract, was hired out by father as field laborer

neighboring farms and plantations. Age 14 was sold (unconfirmed) into concubinage with Tigrynian chieftain, now deceased. Fled his entourage following year in Addis Ababa. Subject harbored at Mission of the Sacred Heart School 16 months, then moved about Ethiopia for three years. Is known to have resided in Dire Dawa, Jima, Gondar. Was occasionally employed housekeeping departments numerous hotels and attended various schools. History this period incomplete. While in Jima, subject implicated in Brighton-Smith incident, but no charges filed. British legation employe James Brighton-Smith convicted smuggling leopard skins out of country. Murder charges dropped re. death of two Ethiopian nationals allegedly involved in scheme. Subject ventured to Asmara in company of Jerome Acton, then USAID employe. Acton recommended subject for employment at Kagnew. Acton is son of Congressman Walter Sanford Acton.

The dossier left many shadows in her history. Durell wondered where the dark alleys of her past had led. He had no way of knowing what sinister affiliations she might have developed. Now it would suit his purposes better if she had gone over to the other side—she was exposed like a loose thread which would unravel the whole fabric of the opposition if pulled.

He had his fingers on that thread and he intended to pull it.

The customer left within the minute. Durell did not turn around. He was aware of the tap of Mira's slippers on the floor, then her husky voice at his back. "May I help you?" she asked in Italian.

He turned around and dangled the numbered locker tab in front of her. "You can welcome me back from the dead—Sheba."

Her eyelashes fluttered and Durell recognized the chaotic look of a reeling mind. Then it was his turn to be surprised.

"Cajun, baby! You're alive!" she cried. She threw her small, firm arms around his neck. Durell did not buy it. He grabbed one arm and peeled her away and saw confusion in her eyes.

"I guess you're not accustomed to rejection," he breathed half to himself as he pushed her roughly toward the front door. She struggled, twisted, yanked to free her arm and almost upset a rack of dresses.

"Look what you're doing! Turn me loose!" Her dark irises flashed.

Durell pressed the button on the door's lock and its steel bolt shot into place. He jerked the curtain down, then shoved her half a step ahead of him toward the back of the store. She wriggled, made a feral sound, aimed her long, red fingernails at his face. Durell easily slapped the hand away. He wrenched her arm behind her back and pushed her fist high between her shoulder blades. She gave a cry of pain.

"Don't fight me, then."

She cursed at him in several languages. They barged through a cloth curtain, past a couple of dressing rooms and into a stockroom. Piles of dresses awaited labeling there. Price tags, bits of cardboard, snips of thread and shipping cartons littered the floor.

A pair of scissors gleamed on a sewing table.

Mira snatched them and swung their deadly point backwards toward a place just under his ribs. Durell stepped aside, chopped lightly at her wrist and the scissors clattered to the floor. At the same instant, she twisted around, teeth bared, and aimed her knee at his groin.

He could have ended it at any moment, but he had not wanted to damage her. Now he lost patience. He moved around the kick, clutched her shoulders and lobbed her against the wall. A framed photo of Naples sprang from the plaster and crashed onto the floor. Mira's eyes went cloudy, reminding Durell of the eyes of a wounded panther, dazed but dangerous. The bow holding her knit top together had come loose. The half-open garment revealed a large share of her deeply cleft breasts. They were riding in a shallow black bra. It looked much too small.

Durell kept his distance.

"Now we will talk," he said.

10

"Honest, Sam, there was a shark."

"And you were shooting at it instead of me."

"I think I got it."

As Durell weighed her words, he considered her face. It was a mask of candor. It reminded him of the expression of a first-rate call girl in the initial moments of an encounter before she started talking business.

They were above the shop, in her apartment. It was done in the dark, violent hues of Africa, scorched browns, visceral reds. There were chubby Gold Coast statues and slit-eyed ceremonial masks; shining Coptic icons and Ethiopian paintings in casein and ink on parchment. The furniture was cheap and eclectic. Durell judged that it had been picked up at auctions and junk shops. It ran to heavy, knobby legs and fat, sodden velour cushions. There were glittering bead curtains and dozens of leafy plants. The place had the intimacy of a hideaway.

He had locked the doors, the one from the stockroom that opened onto the kitchen and another from the street that was the main entrance. Mira had claimed there was no ceiling entrance. He had checked anyway, but found none.

They were calmer now, Durell standing, Mira sitting on a short, bulky couch. She curled a leg under her and her russet skirt slid back along her thigh. She did not pull it down.

"And you just happened to have a high-powered rifle handy," he said.

"Sure. Everybody's scared of the sharks at Massawa, but it's the only beach we have. Lots of people carry guns in their boats in case someone is attacked."

"And then you copped out, ran away. You were only a few yards from me."

"No, baby, you've got it all wrong. It was crazy to stay.

Dodging bullets isn't my line of work. You people pay me for information—and you don't pay enough at that. I don't have to bring back any heads, and I don't want anyone taking mine. I did the best I could, but when you went under, I got the hell out of there. I tell you, I was scared out of my tree—weren't you?"

"I wasn't anything. I was dead." Durell figured she had acquired the slang from American servicemen at Kagnew. It had a certain charm, combined with her thick Italian accent. But he was not charmed.

The soft candlefire came and went in her eyes with her frequent changes of mood. Now it was gone. Her dark almond eyes were black holes from which no light escaped, blacker than interstellar space, revealing nothing. Durell sensed that she was waiting for a clue, something in his expression, a sigh, a change of posture, to tell her where she stood with him. He waited and watched her, not moving a muscle. He decided that she was too strong to have surrendered to the grip of mindless terror. She'd been frightened, yes. But he had learned long ago that one could work with fear, and she had refused to. Maybe she had not tried to kill him, but she had chosen to leave him to die. He would not forget.

Finally, she lost patience. "Look, it's over now," she said.

"It isn't over. You blew the most important task of your career."

"All right, what are you going to do about it?" she demanded.

Durell did not speak for a moment. Then he said evenly, "I'll have to think about that."

Something in the quiet tone of his voice, his dark gaze frightened her as she had never been frightened before, even at the Villa d'Este. He saw it in the way her lips fell apart and her fingernails dug into the arm of the couch.

A breeze came through an open window, bringing the shuffle of feet, the murmur of many voices from the street below. There came a brief strain played on a one-string *masenko* and the cry of a mullah calling the faithful to prayer. The smells of manure, sun-heated stone, flaming eucalyptus resin mixed dimly in Durell's awareness with the sweet, light scent of Mira's perfume.

He did not want to harm her.

With the exception of Hennessey, she might be his only ally in this country of seventy languages and more land area than France, Spain and Portugal combined.

He reminded himself that she would not have been employed by K Section if she had not conformed to the minimum requirements of psychological profiles carefully developed through years of painstaking research. She had a good record, and it included some sensitive jobs, like penetrating the Russian facility near Kagnew. She regularly dated one of its administrators and the intelligence flowed. She had tipped K Section in advance of the first Eritrean Liberation Front attack on Kagnew—and where she had gleaned that information was still a mystery. The desk-bound iron-heads at Defense had ignored her warning. The price had been two Americans taken hostage.

She was an asset and she was a liability. Durell could not judge which was the greater.

"Stop looking at me like that," she said.

"How was I looking at you?"

"I didn't like it."

"Why did Hennessey come here?"

"You saw him? He's supposed to replace you."

"You reported me dead?" He remembered the workboat he had seen dragging the Dahlac passage. He had wondered if it were searching for his body.

"I had to. There certainly was no reason to believe you were still alive."

"How did you know it was me?"

"I wasn't sure at first, but you looked like you could be an American, and I saw your red bathing trunks. I wasn't positive until I went back to the Villa d'Este, after the ELF had gone. I knew the military would come soon, so I had to work fast. The place was a horrible sight. Blood and bodies everywhere. Since I had rented your locker for you, I knew where to look. Your passport was there and so was your gun, wrapped up in your clothes. Then I was just sure you were dead. I brought your things

58

back with me—it wouldn't do for the authorities to find them and start making inquiries."

"Okay." Durell relaxed a bit. He was relieved to have his gun and passport back. The mission had been botched in the beginning, but maybe they could make a fresh start. He said, "I suppose you gave Hennessey the information you were to have given me before all hell broke loose."

"Of course. I had been alerted to expect him."

"Tell me what it was."

Mira paused. Then she said, "I'm a working girl with a business to run. I didn't expect to have to deal with two K Section spooks at the same time. How about a bonus?"

So they weren't starting fresh. Another roadblock. Durell could understand her concern for money—probably she had not felt financially secure for a whole day in her life. But he did not allow that to change his thinking—he had a right to the information, and if he paid her now, there would be no end to it. "Don't haggle with me. Uncle Joe takes care of you regularly," he said bluntly.

She stirred and her skirt hiked up another inch along her thigh. "Can't we find a way to get along together?" she asked.

"I don't have time to look for one. Just do your job." Durell realized she was a woman who could not feel secure with a man unless she had him in sexual thrall.

"You're a good-looking guy," she said in a low voice.

"The information. Now," Durell said urgently.

She glared. "If that's the way you want it. All I know is that Abegas Tessema, a charter pilot, was flying Ineyu the day he disappeared. Ineyu told him to let me know, but he sent some peasant who was coming to market, and I couldn't make much of it. He doesn't have a telephone."

"Nothing about how it happened?"

"No, just that they were together. The messenger said I was to go to Tessema, but I decided to wait for you."

Durell nodded thoughtfully. It was time to contact Washington.

The door to Sheba's control was in a linen closet between the bedroom and kitchen. Mira removed stacks of towels and took out the middle shelf, revealing a wooden button. She pressed it and a spring-loaded door swung open with the remaining shelves still attached to its back. Inside was a small, airless closet. Mira pulled a hanging cord and a bare lightbulb illuminated dusty cartons of books and bric-a-brac.

"I think it was used for smuggling," she said. "It was weeks before I noticed that the kitchen is not as wide as it should be and realized there had to be a hidden space. I kept looking until I found a way in."

A huge Victorian wardrobe of solid oak stood against a wall. Old dresses and coats filled its rack and shoes and shoeboxes were piled haphazardly in the bottom. Mira scooped them onto the floor and raised the bottom panel. A GK 12 transceiver lay there, face-up.

It was smashed beyond repair, as if someone had used a baseball bat on it.

"When could it have happened?" Durell asked.

"It must have been last night. I had an engagement and was out of the apartment."

"Between what hours?"

"Well!"

"All night, then?"

"It's none of your business."

Durell sighed. "It doesn't matter." He was sure that no ordinary hoodlum had done this, not even for hire. It had taken the guts and training of a professional to get into the apartment and find the hidden door—all done without leaving a mark while under constant threat of discovery.

"I don't like the way things are shaping up," Mira said.

"That makes two of us."

She moved close to him, tentatively, like an animal that might accept food from your hand in the winter snows, but was not tame. Durell sensed her desire for protection.

"Get my things," he said. The best way—the only way —that any of them could be safe would be through the success of his mission. He had to make sure that the devil's light never shone again.

Mira brought his things in a bundle from the bedroom.

Durell pocketed his wallet and passport. The snub-nosed .38 S&W felt cool and reliable in his hand as he checked its chamber. It was still fully loaded. He transferred a handful of spare cartridges from the suit jacket Mira had brought to the coat he wore, then slid the pistol into the waistband of his trousers.

"Now tell me where to find this pilot, Tessema," he said. "I want to see him immediately."

When Mira had related the unfamiliar road names and landmarks, Durell hesitated beside the door and regarded the fiery, self-reliant woman for a last moment. "You showed initiative and common sense in bringing my things here," he said. "If they had been found—anywhere—suspicions might have been aroused. It's imperative that I stay clear of the Ethiopian authorities. If they get in the way of my assignment . . ."

He did not finish the sentence.

If that happened, it could mean disaster for mankind. But that was more than Sheba was supposed to know.

11

Durell drove north toward Keren, dodg-ing ragged scars where the natives had dug up asphalt to burn for fuel. Whistling kite hawks circled over the fields of teff; bishop birds with scarlet wing patches darted among the heavy heads of grain. Here and there were the somber remains of a village smashed by bombs or artillery in the government's increasingly ferocious campaign against the ELF.

Durell regretted that Hennessey had got ahead of him. Going separately to the little airstrip where Tessema was quartered doubled the chances of being followed there. He glanced back down the highway in his rear-vision mirror. Traffic was light. He did not think he was being tailed.

He and Hennessey could work together, Durell reflected as the kilometers sped past and the small farms became fewer, more scattered. Mira was something else.

She had more questions to answer, questions about the monarchists, the funds Ambaw and Deste had said they received through Sheba and Ineyu. But that could wait. It was secondary to finding Ineyu and the source of the outlaw atomic blast.

The clock was running on that.

Precious time already had been lost.

The sense of urgency became stronger as Durell stopped and allowed a string of tawny, snapping camels to cross the road. After that, he drove faster until he came to a dirt track and followed it west into the brassy glare of the lowering sun.

The countryside was wilder here. Dry hills thrust whitely at the sky like monstrous bones. Signs of habitation were rare. Stone *tukuls* stood square with small, high windows and tin roofs for defense against *Shifta* bandits, who would burn the roofs if they could and take the people as they ran out.

The BMW bumped across the railroad tracks to Agordat, wound into a cleft between the rocks, and descended toward the airstrip. It was primitive, small and very private—the kind smugglers like, Durell thought. Gullied hills dotted with candelabra cactus surrounded it on three sides and on the fourth, to the west, was the Anseba River. The river was shallow now. High trees and thick brush along its banks drooped under the relentlessly hammering sun.

Someone had moved the biggest stones from the landing strip and piled them at intervals along the runway like a row of nameless graves. Heat waves rippled along the low roof of a corrugated metal hangar nearby. The mud-brick lean-to on its rear would be the pilots' quarters, Durell decided.

Hennessey's Volvo was parked in the shade beside the hangar.

A big Mercedes was just pulling away—too hurriedly, Durell thought. The glare silvered its tinted windows. He could see nothing inside the car.

He gripped the BMW's steering wheel tightly, stamped

on the accelerator. The car jounced eagerly down the rutted track, raising a dust plume that rolled away toward the river in the breeze.

The rear tires of the Mercedes spun and sent up gouts of dirt as its driver saw the plunging BMW and tried too late to cut around it.

Durell swallowed on a tight place in his throat, jerked the steering wheel to the right and locked the brake pedal against the floorboard. The BMW heaved broadside with a loud rasp of gravel, bounced hard, swayed and came to rest, blocking the road in a swirl of grit. The Mercedes veered, buried its bumper in a ditch. Its motor roared crazily as the heavy car became stuck in the rough to the right of the BMW.

He was halfway out of his car when a fist gripping blue steel reached into the sunlight; the BMW's door-mirror shattered beside his elbow. Doors sprang open on the Mercedes. The big, black car was packed with men.

It was fifty feet to the hangar.

Durell fired on the run, heard the bullet smack metal, then threw himself to the ground and rolled as slugs soughed through the space he had just occupied. He jumped up, cut sharply to the left and dived behind the hangar.

Over the harsh sound of his breath, he could hear the men's voices as they came down the slope after him. They would not leave now until they had tried to dig him out, he decided. Maybe they had Tessema and Hennessey.

Or maybe they had left them dead.

In either case, he had stopped them long enough to find out.

Durell held his .38 at the ready and ran through the oven heat radiating from the sunny hangar wall. Indistinct words of command came on the wind. He had to get into the lean-to before they cut him off. He rounded the rear of the hangar, slammed his shoulder against the wooden door of the pilots' quarters and tumbled inside as a slug kicked clods from the mud brick beside his head.

It took a moment for Durell's eyes to accustom themselves to the shadows. Light and air squeezed into the room through one small window and the place smelled of excrement. There were spiders in glossy nests along the bare beams supporting the tin roof. Soiled clothing and dirty eating utensils littered the room. Durell saw that a metal door led through the back wall into the hangar.

Hennessey was sprawled on his face.

Near his head was an enameled chamber pot half full of feces and urine. Blue flies droned around the pot and fed at the red ooze clotting on Hennessey's cotton hair.

Durell glanced out the window, then knelt over the big man. The blood seeped from a crease atop an angry knot on the back of his head. Durell shook him and rolled him over.

"Hennessey?"

The Cairo Central sat up, his lips loose and pink. "Oh, geez," he groaned. He put his hand gingerly to the back of his skull, then looked with distaste at the sticky blood on his fingers. "Cajun? I thought . . ."

"I'm not dead yet."

"They took Tessema," Hennessey said.

"They're just outside. They don't have him for keeps yet."

"One of the bastards zonked me. But good."

"You'll live."

"Don't try to be funny." The North Carolina accent in Hennessey's gravelly voice always was strong, but now he sounded as if he had just come out of the Smokies for the first time. He hauled himself onto an iron cot. "I feel sick to my stomach."

Durell heard the shuffle of feet. They were just beyond the door. He looked around the room and considered the situation. The mud walls provided good protection. The place was like a fort—but they were trapped in it.

"I couldn't help it," Hennessey said. "Three of them came busting through the door."

"These things happen."

"They had the drop on me."

"Forget it; you're lucky to be alive."

"You in there—throw out your weapons and surrender. This is your only chance." The man spoke English with a French, perhaps Corsican accent.

Durell exchanged glances with Hennessey. "Some

chance," he muttered. He moved to the front of the room, jerked the door half-open and saw a man a few feet away. His pistol cracked once and a dark spot broke the flesh between the man's eyes. Blood and bone splinters blasted from the back of his skull; he fell stiffly.

Gunfire clamored from several directions as Durell jerked his hand back and kicked the door closed with his foot. The fusillade continued. Dishes splintered and crashed down from a wall shelf. A coffee pot on the iron stove clanged and wobbled crazily. Dust puffed from the clay walls in a suffocating storm.

When it was over the top half of the door looked mauled as though with axes.

Durell sucked on a bullet crease across his forearm. Hennessey was sitting against a wall, watching him. "They got my gun," he said simply.

"We'll wait until dark," Durell said. The flies buzzed in the chamber pot. The wind whispered under the eaves. Despite the stench of feces, Durell detected a faint pine scent baking out of the timbers above. He shifted his gun for a moment and dried his right palm on his trousers. Then he heard a metallic clumping overhead.

"They're on the roof," Hennessey said, turning his big, granite face upward.

Immediately, Durell said, "I smell gasoline."

"It's coming from the stove."

Resin-colored liquid was gushing through the grating onto the plank floor. Durell knew they must be pumping it from the aircraft storage tank he had seen next to the wall.

"Into the hangar!" he ordered. He jerked the metal door open and leaped into the dusky building, Hennessey at his heels. Durell slammed the door shut and threw the lock.

"Those bastards," Hennessey growled.

"Stay back from the wall." The lean-to was like a bomb now, and Durell expected it to go off any minute.

Shadow muddied everything in the windowless building. Thin blades of light thrust beneath a side entrance and big, counterweighted doors at the front. Aircraft parts and tools littered work benches. The air was heavy with the smell of engine oil.

The hangar was large enough to house a couple of small planes, but a four-seater Beechcraft was the only one there.

An explosion thundered against the wall. The door to the lean-to burst open and flame erupted twenty feet into the hangar, suffusing the air with stinging vapors. Debris rattled onto the roof.

Quickly, Durell shouldered the warped steel door closed. The lean-to's walls were gone, its floor a gasoline-fed inferno.

Then Hennessey said: "We might have had a chance with the Beechcraft—but if Tessema's alive, it would mean leaving without him."

They looked wordlessly at each other, the tension drawing their lips tight.

"When they don't find us in the rubble out there, they'll charge this place," Durell said. He glanced about, wondering if they could move enough stuff to form a barricade in a corner. It was no use; the work benches were bolted to the walls.

"Give me your gun, and I'll draw their fire to the side door," Hennessey said. "You can squeeze under the front doors and see if Tessema is still in their car. If he is, get him and get the hell out of here."

"I'm not leaving you."

"Tessema is the whole show, Sam. He's what we came for, but only one of us is going to get away with him."

Durell knew that Hennessey's reasoning was sound. He was being very professional; Tessema was the objective. Only he could forward the mission.

"What's it going to be, Cajun? Time's running out."

When Durell did not answer, Hennessey sighed. "Maybe you've been in the business too long, old pal. Maybe you should stay and cover me. At least you'd go down in style. If I make it this way, I'll have to report how you handled it. They'll put you out to pasture. You won't like it."

Durell ignored him, got up and poked around the hangar until he found what he was looking for—a chest containing emergency flares and a flaregun, standard equipment at any airstrip.

"I'm going out the side door," he said. "They won't be watching, I hope. When I'm out of sight, shoot off a flare to draw them to this side of the building. Then button up and wait."

"For a miracle, I suppose?"

Durell cracked the door cautiously. The sun had sunk behind the hills and a feverish red afterglow burned in the sky above them. The lavender of deepening twilight welled up in the basin holding the airstrip.

No one was in sight.

Durell figured they were behind the hangar, waiting for the fire to burn itself out. Then they would root through the rubble for the bodies. They would not leave until they were sure of their victims.

He wormed out of the door on his belly. Slowly, gun in hand, he crawled to the front of the hangar and waited. There came the pop of the flaregun and a sparkling red flare arched through the dusk. Durell ran in a low crouch. A fresh highland breeze swirled sparks from the crackling lean-to and the fire's reflection slapped nervously on the windows of the three cars.

He glimpsed the thin, angular silhouette of a man in the Mercedes. That could be Tessema, Durell thought, but it seemed strange that there was no guard on him. If the man in the car was the pilot, then Hennessey had been right—he could get away with Tessema now. Durell did not mean to sacrifice a partner.

He was aware of the continuing racket of gunfire as he ran to the BMW and retrieved the JP plastic explosive and detonator from its trunk. Then he rushed back to the front hangar doors, hefted them a foot and squeezed under.

Bullet holes spotted the hangar walls with dull gray light.

Hennessey lay flat on the ground, dirt sticking to his hair and face. "They're going to come through any minute," he said.

"Get up front," Durell said. "Open the main doors when I give the signal."

Hennessey moved to the hoist cord by the big doors as Durell clambered onto the wing and into the cockpit of the Beechcraft. He worked expertly with the plastic, placing it just inside the pilot's door. Then he slid behind the controls and scanned the instrument panel. The key was in the ignition. He pressed the starter button.

The engine coughed and then churned out a steady blast of sound, throwing a blue mist of flame from its exhaust. The noise was shattering in the confined space of the hangar. The aircraft shuddered and bucked against its brakes.

Durell throttled the engine back to idling speed and stuck the fuses into the doughy mass of plastic. He waved to Hennessey to open the doors. Soft, iron-colored light flooded into the hangar as the doors rose. He released the brakes and leaped from the plane. Bullets screamed past him as he ran toward the deep shadows in the rear. He knew they would go for the plane first.

The aircraft trundled mindlessly out of the hangar.

Durell held his breath and watched the scene play itself out. The men fired madly at the Beechcraft, ripping off shot after shot at its cabin. It struck a bump and angled slightly to the right. They followed it like fish in a net.

One gained the wing on the passenger side, looked through the window and yelled something.

Sweat broke out on Durell's forehead. If they realized the airplane was empty, the trap would not work.

The man on the wing gestured and yanked at the passenger door.

At the same mement, another mounted the opposite wing and jerked open the pilot's door.

Durell winced; the ground heaved; the explosion reverberated across the hills. Bodies spun crazily in the air with chunks of flesh and metal. Cartwheeling wings spewed pinwhells of flaming gasoline, and orange ropes of fire writhed upward in a blossom of gray and black smoke.

A flailing torch ran insanely, cutting one way, then another, and dropped to the ground making the gut noises of a dying animal.

Then the wilderness was quiet.

Durell did not trust it.

Hennessey started to speak, and Durell raised his hand sharply for silence. He waited in the shadows for a full minute, every sense tuned to catch the slightest vibration in air or earth. Then slowly, with expert stealth, he approached the front doorway, peered beyond and stepped cautiously outside.

"They're dead, Sam, all of them," Hennessey said.

"Maybe," Durell said. If even one of the men were left, death could reach out suddenly from almost any point of the compass. He kept his gun at the ready as he went away from the hangar, but no one fired, nothing moved.

He took a deep, shuddering breath of the thin air. It was cool now, at last. In these latitudes, the twilight was brief. Night held the sky in its black grip. Swarms of stars glittered in the tropical heavens and a frail, orange feather lay on the eastern rim where the moon would rise. Durell had been further from home, but nowhere that seemed as unearthly distant.

"The fartherest outpost of mankind . . . the land beyond the sunrise," he murmured.

"What is that?" Hennessey asked.

"Ethiopia, according to Homer."

"Homer can have it."

"Let's get Tessema," Durell said.

12

Now Durell understood why there had been no guard with Tessema.

He was stone blind.

His hands shook violently when Durell opened the door of the Mercedes and he appeared to be on the verge of physical and emotional collapse.

"We're your friends," Durell said. "The others are gone."

"I heard an explosion." Tessema spoke English in a rich Amharic accent, turning his head back and forth.

His features under the dome light were classical Ethiopian: narrow, sensitive face; sharp, prominent nose; thin, strong mouth. One look and Durell saw that he had been barely able to care for himself. Food stains splotched his leather flying jacket, the front of his blue workshirt, even his frayed khaki shorts.

Durell and Hennessey helped him into the BMW, hearing the wary chuckles of hyenas coming down from the hills toward the desolate airstrip. "They'll have a feast tonight," Hennessey said.

"Meet me at Mira's," Durell said.

The two cars pulled away from the airstrip and headed for Asmara. Embers still glowed where the lean-to had been, but the wreckage of the airplane had burned quickly and there was no sign of it in the darkness.

Durell's heart sank as he considered the sightless Tessema. He had been with Ineyu when something had happened to the Ethiopian Central. Durell had hoped the pilot would fly him to the place where that had occurred. Now that was out of the question.

Still, Tessema could point him in the right direction—if he would talk.

"You needn't be frightened," Durell said as they drove through the orange dawning of the moon. The pilot's hands were shaking again.

"I have no fear. Death is a well-trodden path. I can find my way, once I am set upon it. I am merely exhausted. Where are you taking me?"

"Mira Seragate's. Do you know her?"

Tessema was visibly relieved. "No, but Ineyu Worota told me to tell her about our misfortune if he did not return. I sent word to her. She never came."

"I came in her place. Ineyu is my associate. Tell me."

Yellow squares of lamplight floated by as they passed a village. A lace of acacia trees intervened, then dense cedars and the lights disappeared behind them.

Tessema said nothing. Durell did not press him.

They were on the Keren highway now and Durell slowed where a military convoy was parked beside the road. Someone impatiently whirled a flashlight and urged them past a blazing fuel truck. The government was having trouble keeping the highway open, especially at night. The ELF roamed the countryside freely.

"You can have food and rest at Mira's," Durell said.

"Thank you."

Again the silence, the whistle of air against the car, the steady hum of its motor. Lights of Asmara came over a rise in the blacktop.

Finally, Tessema said: "We crash-landed in the mountains."

"Is that how you were blinded?"

"That happened before the crash. We were eighty or ninety kilometers east of Gondar, south of Mount Rasadajan. Suddenly, there was a great white flash of light three or four kilometers ahead of us. I could see nothing after that."

Durell's pulse quickened. *The devil's light.* Tessema had witnessed the atomic blast.

"Ineyu was looking down to the side when it happened. His eyes were unharmed. He helped me get the aircraft down onto a mountain meadow."

"But only you came back. What happened to Ineyu?"

"He went for help. I waited through the night and the next day Geech shepherds found me." Tessema thought for a moment. "The mountains are treacherous. Maybe Ineyu fell from a cliff. Perhaps a leopard got him in a valley forest. Or bandits."

"Were there any landmarks?" Durell asked.

"There was a castle. We passed it a few kilometers north of the explosion. I penciled it onto my map as a checkpoint."

"Where's the map?"

Tessema shook his head. "Ineyu took it."

"Then tell me your airspeed, duration of flight and compass heading. I'll have to plot the location as best I can."

They were in the city now, speeding along a palm-lined thoroughfare as Tessema related the information. Sidewalk cafes sparkled with activity and Durell wondered how long the people could maintain their business-as-usual atmosphere. With the ELF interdicting the highways, the supply problem mounted daily.

"Did Ineyu say anything—anything about the area, what he was doing there?" Durell asked.

"He instructed me to fly over it and return. We weren't to touch down there. He said some company had a mining concession in the vicinity, that he had to find out if they had started construction. We didn't see any evidence of it."

"What was the name of the company?"

Tessema's empty eyes stared without blinking at the oncoming headlights. Then he said, Sinigaglia—Sinigaglia Minerals."

The name struck a response among the numberless bits of data stored in Durell's brain. The recollection faded, sinking back into obscurity, and mentally he lunged for it. Lines of concentration deepened on his tanned forehead as he turned left past an equestrian statue. The car went from the macadam street onto cobblestones and made a washboard sound.

Then Durell remembered. . . .

The mining firm was a subsidiary of Compagnia Sinigaglia Generale, a multibillion-dollar corporation chartered in Italy. Its chairman and principal stockholder was Geza Della Gatta, briefly notorious the decade before for his camera-smashing street bouts with gossip photographers, transatlantic spending sprees and insatiable hunger for power. His stint with the jet set had lasted only a short while, however. Jaded or too busy for that loose agglomeration of the self-indulgent superrich, he had dropped out of sight. For the last five or six years, he had worked his financial wizardry from the sumptuous obscurity affected by many of the world's exceedingly wealthy man. Shielded by highly paid errand boys with imposing titles, veiled behind untold corporate layers, he had become ever more elusive and powerful. His personal worth was estimated at more than one billion dollars.

Durell parked in front of the dress shop. He got out of the car and helped Tessema out, then led him across the pavement by the wrist. A metal shutter had been rolled down to cover the display window. Hennessey was only half a minute behind. Durell pushed the call button beside the door to Mira's apartment, scanned the street in both directions, pressed the button again. The street looked deserted. A distant string of shots sounded from the Arab quarter. Durell figured the police were raiding a suspected ELF hideout, as they did most nights. A fog of insects orbited a street light down on the corner of the block. Bats cut through the swarm, feeding.

"The lights are out; looks like she's gone," Hennessey said. "I'll get the lock."

He took a set of picklocks from his coat pocket and bent to work. Durell heard the tumblers click almost immediately. Hennessey pushed the door open.

"That was quick work," Durell said.

The door at the top of the stairs also was locked. Hennessey had it open in a couple of seconds and the sweet scent of Mira's perfume spilled out of the apartment.

Durell thumbed a wall switch and the lights came on. Nothing appeared to have been disturbed. He nodded to the bedroom. "Check it," he said. Hennessey's big, square frame moved through the bead curtain with a glassy rattle. Durell led Tessema to the couch and went into the kitchen. The table was clean, dirty dishes in the sink. He found lamb chops in the refrigerator and tossed them onto the griddle. While they sizzled, he scrambled a dozen eggs in a big skillet.

"Everything's cool," Hennessey called from the living room. "There's no telling where she went—probably a date."

Durell wasn't so sure; she had been clearly worried when he left her. There was nothing he could do about it now, however, and his mind turned back to Della Gatta.

The man had disappeared during the confusion of World War II, right here in Ethiopia. He was believed to have lived under an assumed name until 1947, when he surfaced in Italy and bought the controlling interest in Sinigaglia Generale Petroli Italiana, then a moribund chemical company.

Where he had obtained the funds for that deal was unknown.

The world's police and intelligence communities suspected the money came from war loot—priceless treasures of church and empire smuggled out of Ethiopia—but that had never been proven.

He must have used large sums to buy information on the Italian economy, Durell reflected, because nobody in his right mind would have invested in the company he bought—unless they had been tipped off about the discovery of the Po Valley gas fields before it was publicly announced the next year. That had turned Sinigaglia into an important producer of chemicals and put Della Batta on the way to his first legitimate wealth.

Then came the acquisition of other companies under the umbrella of Campagnia Sinigaglia Generale as the Marshall Plan pumped billions of U.S. dollars into Europe, and Della Gatta had moved into the front rank of financiers with international influence.

Durell remembered there was another side to the man, even less known and more ominous.

A physicist and head of the corporate laboratories of Corradini Chemicals, Milan, before he was twenty-one, Della Gatta had, on that birthday in 1936, become a member of the *partito Nazionale Fascista*.

He was immediately assigned to the national headquarters staff of the OVRA, Mussolini's secret police. Only weeks later, he had been shipped to Ethiopia and given his own OVRA command. His unit had accompanied Italian troops on their triumphal entry into Addis Ababa in May, 1936.

The next year there had been an attempted assassination of the Italian viceroy, Marshall Granziani. Della Gatta had played an instrumental role in reprisal murders of an estimated 30,000 Ethiopians.

Durell wondered if Della Gatta's ruthless intelligence now dared to warp the world's delicate atomic balance for personal gain.

He had to assume there was no more likely candidate.

"Yes, I've heard of Sinigaglia. You don't think they have anything to do with this, do you?" Hennessey guided a shivering heap of eggs into his mouth. He and Durell were in the kitchen where they could talk apart from the pilot, who ate in the living room.

"Not as a company, of course. But maybe Della Gatta does. He could be using Sinigaglia as a front, just to hold the turf. After all, the event occurred on or near a Sinigaglia mining concession."

"These mineral companies are always speculating in the developing countries," Hennessey said. "They get a mining concession so all the suckers think they've got something hot going. Their stock shoots up and they make a killing and get out before the roof caves in on all of the rich widows and retired school teachers. They don't even have to dig a hole in the ground. I've seen it a million times here in Africa. Let's forget Sinigaglia. Hell, Tessema's given us a rough fix on the location. Let's just get down there and find out who's responsible, whoever the bastards are."

"I'm leaving for Gondar tonight, but it isn't that simple," Durell said. He called to Tessema: "What are the chances of parachuting into the vicinity where Ineyu was lost, Mr. Tessema? Somewhere near the castle. It would have to be done at night to avoid being seen."

"In the thin air at that altitude? With the mountain winds and cliffs and canyons? It would be madness," Tessema called back.

Durell turned to Hennessey. "Then we'll have to hike in. That means guides and provisions for several days. It makes sense for me to go ahead and get started on the arrangements while you finish up here. I want you to radio K Section. Ask for a background on Sinigaglia— any principals, holdings or current projects connected with Ethiopia or atomic energy."

"For a multinational conglomerate?" Hennessey rolled his eyes. "You know what you're asking?"

"Look, Washington can put the information together in a few hours. Most of it will be in the computer bank. The operation may have been pulled out of the mountains by the time we get there—they know we are on their trail. If it has, and Sinigaglia looks suspicious, I can follow it immediately to Italy or wherever the smell leads." Durell frowned. "Sheba's transceiver is busted; you'll have to get yours from the hotel."

They put their empty plates in the sink and walked back to the living room. As they rejoined the blind pilot, Durell said, "Mr. Tessema also must be taken care of—we can't walk off and leave him. When you contact headquarters, tell them to send a party to pick him up at Andrews Air Force Base and take him to a hospital. Maybe his sight can be restored. Get him on a Navy courier plane out of Kagnew before dawn. Then meet me tomorrow afternoon—you know where."

"I guess I'll be up all night," Hennessey said.

"It won't hurt you. Go get your things and bring them here. I'll wait with Mr. Tessema."

"Am I going to America?" Tessema asked, turning his vacant eyes back and forth.

A chuckle rattled in Hennessey's throat. "The big score, old fella. Stateside. Do you have any family here?"

"No," Tessema replied.

"Good," Hennessey said flatly.

"A job will be arranged, whether your sight returns or not," Durell said.

"You are kind," Tessema said quietly.

Durell and Hennessey exchanged knowing glances. The pilot was marked for death unless they got him out of the country. Durell had viewed the matter objectively and concluded that what was worse was what he might say before he died, if the other side got its hands on him. He could reveal merely by the nature of Durell's questions much that the American agents knew and where they were likely to head next.

"It's not a favor," Durell said evenly. "You are in danger here, and that endangers us. We are protecting ourselves."

13

Durell felt grimy and tired as he strode under the old-fashioned ceiling fans in the Ras Hotel lobby. He decided to bathe and catch a couple of hours sleep before heading toward Gondar.

Body heat and tobacco smoke, the mixed scents of perfume, sweat and alcohol clutched at him as he passed the carved mahogany archway leading to the bar. A band from Cairo played loud American numbers and couples bumped each other on the parquet dance floor. B girls worked minor diplomats, Italian planters and military officers for two-dollar glasses of tea. Durell longed for a tall bourbon, but not in there. He got his room key and asked that whiskey, soda and ice be sent to his room.

No one in the lobby appeared to be watching for his arrival. The events of the day left the opposition a bit disorganized, he decided, climbing the stairs to his floor.

Then he noticed that the brown paper tattletale he had stuck in the crack of his door lay on the carpet. Someone had entered his room again. It could have been the maid. Or anybody else.

They could still be in there.

He reached inside his coat and gripped the butt of his .38, warm where it rested against his abdomen under his waist band. A Kenyan in wide, flowing robes walked by and he kept his hand there as they nodded politely to each other. He tested the iron door handle slowly, with extreme care. The door was unlocked. The percussion of the band came vaguely from below like the beat of a savage heart. Durell glanced down the hallway to make sure the Kenyan was gone. The hallway was empty, its gilded mirrors draped in shadows under the low light. Then he drew his pistol and pushed the door open with a rigid forefinger.

A .32 revolver jerked up to point between his eyes.

For the second time in as many days, Mira was holding a gun on him.

A bedside lamp with a brass lion base cast golden straws of light on the barrel of the little pistol, matching the fluttering blaze in her dark, almond eyes.

Durell kicked the door closed with his heel. "Put it down," he said.

"You first, Sam, baby," she replied in a tough, husky voice.

A couple of seconds passed wordlessly as Durell thought

how close he had come to killing her. There had been time to fire before she got the gun out of her lap.

Her shoes were off and her hair was slightly disarrayed, as if she had been lying down. It made her look earthy, provocative. Durell had no difficulty imagining what thoughts must have gone through the Tigrynian chieftain's head as he encountered her shining with sweat in her father's fields.

Maybe he had been wrong not to shoot.

She held her pistol steady, aimed at his head.

He tried not to think what a .32 slug between the eyes might feel like. She could not be any happier about the way his .38 was pointed at the V between her proud breasts.

Moving without haste, he crossed the room and casually grasped her pistol, slipping his finger behind its trigger. She made no move to stop him and released the weapon readily. Durell's instinct had been right. He let out his breath.

"You scared the hell out of me," she said.

"Consider yourself lucky," he said angrily. "What were you doing with this thing?" He dropped the gun into a crocodile handbag lying next to the bed.

"I didn't know who might come through the door. I've been waiting two hours. The bellboy let me in. I told him I was your—lady." A wry twist crossed her lips.

Durell replaced his pistol under his belt, laid his dusty jacket across the foot of the bed and collapsed onto a straw chair.

"You shouldn't be here," he said. He rubbed his blood-shot eyes and had a vision of the hyenas coming down to the mutilated flesh scattered on the airstrip.

"I'm always somewhere I shouldn't be. Or with some-one I shouldn't be with. It's my business, remember?"

"Just so long as you remember," he said.

They regarded each other as the sound of a radio announcer speaking in vibrant Amharic tones came from a room down the hall. Footfalls padded by on the thick carpet outside the door. Durell turned his eyes away to the window and saw the Coptic church on its moonlit hill, a large mosque just below it.

His shoulder ached. He had a thousand things on his mind. The affair at the airstrip had been just for starters. He hoped that Tessema would reach Kagnew without interference and get safely out of the country—if anything went wrong, it could mean the loss of Hennessey as well.

Dejasmatch Ambaw and Deste, the French girl with noble Ethiopian blood, should be on their way to the mountains now, provided they had slipped past the police and had not run afoul of the ELF. Durell figured their chances of recapturing the dead emperor's kingdom were nil. The people were fed up with the corruption and oppression of an ancient regime that favored the Amhara minority and had not been able even to stamp out the slave trade until 1964. The monarchist crusade would have been laughable, had it not implied more killing and destruction for the future.

Then there was the mysterious Geza Della Gatta, his whereabouts—his intentions.

And an atomic plague ten times more deadly than the Black Death of the Middle Ages that could come like doomsday at any time.

Finally, there was Durell's own survival—not an easy matter when a bellboy might let any stranger into his room merely for the asking. . . .

"Why did you come?" he asked.

She swung her lovely legs off of the bed in a motion as graceful as it was revealing. Her voice was low but strong with the tension in her. "I felt bad about the way things went between us at my place. I came to set them right, Sam, baby."

"They're all right," Durell said tonelessly.

A smile came to her pouting lips and she moved onto the arm of his chair. The straw of the chair made punished, snapping sounds under her light body as she leaned toward him.

"We could make them better," she said.

"You're using your sex like an iron mace, Mira."

She made an amused sound deep in her throat, but there was something like anger in her smoky eyes. Durell sud-

79

denly realized that she did not like men; did not like needing them.

Then she pressed the weight of her breasts against his chest and put her lips close to his, and she said, "But didn't you know? Sex has always been a weapon. Let's make war."

Durell later realized that his mind had been somewhat confused at the moment. When he heard the door open, he assumed it was room service bringing the whiskey he had ordered. Then he saw the look on Mira's face as she glanced beyond his shoulder and all the warm tinglings that had started turned into icicles in his guts.

He twisted and glimpsed a disappearing flash of brown skin. At the same instant, he heard a thump on the floor and caught sight of something wobbling past the chair and recognized with dismay the deeply notched form of a fragmentation-type hand grenade.

Adrenaline shot through his fibers and launched him out of the chair and he spilled Mira onto the floor. She scrambled on all fours for the back of the bed as Durell scooped up the heavy lump of cold metal and tossed it expertly.

It sailed through the open bathroom door and splashed into the bowl of the big, old-fashioned water closet.

He dived behind the bed. The floor kicked him in the stomach as giant hands slapped his ears. Lamps toppled. Walls and ceiling hurled a blizzard of plaster and white dust.

They were not harmed. Durell saw that the blast had cracked the old commode, but it was still standing. It had focused the force of the explosion upward and what was left of the bathroom ceiling hung in splinters.

He ran into the hallway, aware of the murmur of alarmed voices, heads poking out of doors. The stairwell exit was just closing.

Then he was on the stairs, gun held in loose, competent fingers. He heard the soft slap of sneakers rapidly descending down below. He started down, taking two, three steps at a time, every sense alert.

The sound of the sneakers stopped.

Durell waited at a turning, listening, arm cocked so that the .38 was pointed upward beside his shoulder. Each flight of the stairs was walled; you couldn't see the flight below. Still no footfalls. He thought he heard a distant rasp of heavy breathing, but he was not sure.

Quickly he rounded the next corner, bounded halfway down the flight and drew up short. A wiry youth, yellow oiling the whites of his frightened eyes, stepped abruptly into sight and flung a dagger at his chest. Durell evaded the knife, heard it *ping* against the wall behind him and triggered a shot at the man's left thigh. But the youth moved too fast and was almost out of sight around the next turn before the knife had clattered onto the stairs.

Most young fellows of this kind would have waited to see the result of the throw. This one was smarter than that. Durell darted down after him once more, hoping he could get a clean shot at a leg or arm. He wanted to use only enough force to stop him.

What he knew was much more important to Durell than taking his life.

He came to the bottom landing. From here half a flight of worn marble steps descended into the lobby, where he hoped he would not have to go. He judged that his assailant would avoid that, too.

He heard footsteps coming from above.

Something caught his eyes through a small window in double doors to his right. It was the youth, dressed in a faded brown suit, darting across the empty expanse of a dimly lighted ballroom. Durell burst into the huge, gloomy space and aimed carefully. The figure ran frantically toward a back exit on the left side of an electronic organ. Durell led the target slightly, tensed his finger evenly on the trigger . . .

An arm knocked the gun down and the wasted shot echoed through the cavernous chamber, its slug ripping a hole in the polished wooden floor.

A hotel employe jabbered something in an unfamiliar dialect, wrestled at Durell's arm. Durell yanked loose, swept his elbow back hard and floored the man just as the youth dashed through the exit.

Durell ran after him and came out in an alley. Sour

garbage and the carcass of a dead animal flooded the narrow way with a nose-stopping stench. The moon's rays did not penetrate here.

Durell moved quickly and silently, for all his size. The man he sought was somewhere in the darkness ahead. He had not had time to get out of the alley. Durell would see him against the faint shine of the moon at its end, when he tried.

The night was not alien to Durell. Years of experience had suited him to function as well as any man could in its shadows and he exercised to perfection the technique of watching out of the light-sensitive corners of his eyes while every intinct demanded that he look straight at what he wanted to see. He strode relentlessly up the alley, expecting the nerve of his quarry to break at any moment, then flushed him about twenty yards away.

The man darted for the street opening, his coat flapping, his baggy, shapeless pants grabbing at his ankles. Durell moved to the middle of the alley and steadied his pistol in both hands. It was a difficult shot, given the distance, the lack of illumination. He took his time, squeezed the trigger and saw the flare of the muzzle flame.

The target staggered and fell.

Durell ran toward him as he struggled upright and hobbled around the corner into the street. The man could not go far and it would be simple to spot him. He would be easy to take now.

Durell wondered if it were only his own footfall that he heard through the sound of his breath and the vast sighing of the city. He glanced back and saw nothing. He did not slow down.

He pushed his gun into his pants pocket as he entered the street. It was dirty and narrow, not much more appealing than the alley. Casual refuse littered its stones and flies crawled sluggishly on the walls in the night chill. Raucous music, Ethiopian and American, struck at his ears.

There were small neon signs advertising the more prosperous bars. Tin signs, lighted with incandescent bulbs, marked dingy *talla* houses, where Durell glimpsed men with less money to spend sipping barley *talla* from horns and a mead called *tedj* from long-necked flasks. Fences made of rusty tin sheeting separated some of the structures. Men in twos and threes moved from bar to bar; haggled with harlots standing by the doors. They were the only women in sight. Most of them were young and beautiful.

Durell saw his man drag himself into a doorway beneath a sign for Melotti beer. He sensed the danger in there. He might well be surrounded by the man's accomplices, maybe get a knife between the shoulder blades. These squalid streets and dens clearly comprised the natural habitat of the man who had tried to kill him. It was doubtful that he had ever been in the Ras before tonight.

But Durell had to find out who sent him. And the only way was to go in after him.

He took a short, deep breath and stepped through the green-painted threshold. The smell of malt, vomit and the rancid butter with which Ethiopians plastered down their hair assaulted his nostrils. Dim, aqueous light from a fixture in the center of the low ceiling struck people and tables and cast spokes of shadow outward on the rough-planked floor.

The man he had followed was not visible anywhere.

From where Durell stood, spots of dark blood traced his path along the front of the bar and then into a dusky alcove with doors on either side. It was only about forty feet, but it seemed like a mile.

Iron stares probed him. All conversation had stopped when he entered, and there was no music. The silence was almost palpable, a barricade they dared him to cross.

Durell returned the stares evenly. No one challenged the big muscular man.

In the unnatural silence he moved down the narrow bar along the trail of blood. He was almost to the alcove when a woman in a flimsy print dress swayed seductively toward him. Heavy rouge marred the perfect skin of her chestnut face. He waved her away, started to step around her. She moved to block his path.

"Pardon me, I have business in the restroom," he said.

"You like me?" She grinned.

"Yes. Excuse me, please." He sensed someone coming up behind him. The woman did not move, her expression did not change. At least a couple of men were at his back now. He could feel them there without having to look. Another moved across the periphery of his vision and out of sight to his rear.

Durell brushed the woman roughly aside and strode toward the alcove.

He felt someone grab his shoulders from behind, whirled, brought his forearm savagely around in front of him and felt its solid impact as two of the men staggered into the bar and fell. Another hit him in the stomach. He hardly felt it in all the tumult and floored him with a chop to the side of the neck, aware of the woman pummeling his back and men yelling in rage.

Then something like a stick of dynamite went off in his left kidney and he dropped to one knee, the pain half-paralyzing him. Grimy hands dug at his face, fingers gouged his neck, blows struck him everywhere. He raised up somehow, hauling two men off of their feet, and lashed out with his fists, elbows and knees at the suffocating mass of flesh enveloping him.

The sheer weight of his opponents dragged him down and he tasted blood on his tongue. His hand dug for the pistol.

He threw them off long enough to struggle up once more and slammed the pistol backhand into the face of one diving for him.

There were three still on their feet in front of his gun, frozen, crouched, waiting.

And something very sharp bit the skin between his shoulder blades.

He knew the point of a knife when he felt one.

They took him into the alcove and opened the door where the blood trail led. The muzzle of a French-made MAB automatic pistol was waiting there, its butt resting on the crazed varnish of a table next to a bottle of grappa.

The man holding the gun said: "*Bonsoir, Monsieur* Durell." Then, curtly, "Bring him in."

It was the same Corsican voice that had demanded Durell's surrender at the airstrip.

14

The man Durell had followed was on the

floor in a corner of the room, slumped against a stack of beer cases. His trouser leg was sodden with blood around the calf, but the wound could have been worse. If Durell's bullet had struck the bone he could never have left the alley.

The Corsican laid Durell's snub-nosed pistol on the table, next to a fragile glass that held his drink of grappa. Then he ordered the others out of the room. They wanted money. "You will be paid. Get out," he said. They looked at the 9mm MAB and left sullenly.

After they closed the door, he sneered, "Trash. African trash."

His hot, rapacious gaze had not once left Durell. His dark eyes gleamed from a flat, pugnacious face beneath a cap of black hair shining with perfumed pomade. He wore an ivory-colored suit of tropical-weight material and an Alpha cigarette burned in an ebony holder that he gripped between the thumb and forefinger of his left hand. "Sit down," he ordered.

Durell did as he was told, regarded the man with practiced eyes and decided he was wary but unafraid, fully professional. There was an aura of danger about him, utterly amoral and callous.

"So, the charm is broken," the Corsican said. "You have been most fortunate—up to now."

"I die hard."

"I am in a position to find out first-hand, am I not?"

Durell made no reply. He noticed a door beside the table. There was a window in it and he saw that it led outside. He began calculating how to get to it. The only weapons he could bring to bear were his intelligence and experience and will. Possibly they were superior to the Corsican's, but you didn't take anything for granted.

The will was the most fundamental at the moment—the will to kill versus the will to survive.

Durell seemed to have the upper hand there. Already the Corsican had hesitated to kill him for an eternity of seconds, and every fraction counted in the struggle of minds and wills. Durell did not understand why, but the Corsican was reluctant to trigger the one deadly blast it would take to eliminate him. The man could be under orders to hold him for someone, deliver him somewhere, but Durell sensed it was something deeper, something in the character of the man himself. The reason, whatever it might be, was Durell's strength. If he could isolate it, he might use it to lever the man off balance for one critical moment.

The thoughts bruised through Durell's mind all in an instant, but the message was clear and urgent—survival would be by the slimmest of margins, if at all. To attain it, he would have to wage and win a psychological battle.

Durell saw that the Corsican savored his command of the situation as he allowed a suggestion of amusement to twist a corner of his thin lips. He was in no hurry. Dogs barked to each other through the squalid quarter. A rooster crowed at the moon. Muffled voices of strumpets and their patrons came and went from beyond the door.

"You have Ineyu Worota?" Durell asked.

"I see that Mr. Tessema told you of their unfortunate mishap," the Corsican said smugly.

"He's still alive?"

"It's of no consequence to you, of course, but yes, he still lives. His fate is out of your hands—as is your own."

Relief for the Ethiopian Central flooded through Durell. If Ineyu could get free, the information he brought out of the mountains would be invaluable.

He continued to probe the Corsican. "You arranged to have the plastic explosive placed in my car?"

"*Oui.* Your use of it in the aircraft today was most ingenious. I must compliment you."

"I wonder if the men who died out there would share your sporting attitude."

The Corsican gave a Gallic shrug. "Africans, all of them. Ignorant. Hardly more than savages. I am familiar with their kind, from the Congo to Algeria, where they put many of my comrades in unmarked graves. They kill like dogs and they die like dogs. They have no sensibilities, no appreciation for the culture that we Europeans attempted for over a hundred years to give them."

"You asked a high price for your culture."

The Corsican smiled. "You Americans are so naïve, so simple. That is why I sit here as the victor; you are humbled as the vanquished." His gun still pointed at Durell's chest. It never wavered.

The bleeding man whimpered. His face was ashen. The Corsican seemed not to notice.

"Maybe you're a coward," Durell said. "I didn't see you at the airstrip. You let your men take all the risks, just like him." He nodded toward the man in the corner.

The Corsican did not take his feverish eyes off of Durell. "On the contrary. I am a general, you see, and they say a good general is worth a division of men. He does not expose himself to capture or death." He sipped the grappa from the thin-shelled glass. "Perhaps you have heard of me. I am Joseph Cesari."

Pride.

There was a weakness that could be exploited, Durell thought. The man simply wanted to impress him. He had a swollen ego, inflamed with arrogance and doubtlessly very tender. Durell recognized the name—the French Sûreté had kept it on Interpol lists for years.

"I've never heard of you," he said blandly.

Cesari's thin brows knotted together. "Most strange for a man of your experience, *Monsieur* Cajun. Well, it is fitting that you should know who has bested you before you die. As an officer of the Tenth Parachute Division, I fought for the generals in Algeria when they revolted against the treasonous French government in 1961. Naturally, I was a member of the Secret Army Organization better known as the OAS. I was one of those who ambushed General Charles De Gaulle at Petit-Clamart. He narrowly escaped, you know. I fought as a mercenary in Katanga and later, under Premier Tshombe, in the Congo. My services are widely sought—and expensive."

"You were on the wrong side every time, Cesari. You're a loser."

The short, sleek man rose angrily to his feet and leveled the big MAB at Durell's breastbone. "I am on the winning side now, *monsieur*."

The muscles in Durell's jaw knotted. He did not think it would be long now, one way or the other. He kept talking. "You mean the atom project? You are a ridiculous, stupid little man, Cesari. If that is successful, there won't be any winners."

"Oh, yes," Cesari panted. "It is nearly completed now. Two days? A week? Then no one in the world can stop us."

"Who hired you, Cesari? Was it Geza Della Gatta?" Durell watched closely, but the name brought no reaction to Cesari's face.

"Do you really think I would tell you?" he asked.

"Why not, if you're going to murder me anyway?"

"Please, such a question is patronizing. Let us talk as equals."

"We're not equals."

"I have conquered you, Cajun—you must respect me for that. Just be thankful that you die at meritorious hands."

"I'm not thankful."

"Perhaps I will spare you, if you beg."

"No, you won't."

Cesari's cheeks tightened into flat boards and he threw his cigarette holder onto the table. He swilled a slug of grappa around inside his mouth and suddenly sprayed it in Durell's face. Durell winced and wiped the cheap, stinging liquor from his eyes as Cesari gave a mad, high laugh.

"Now toast me!" he cried. "Toast the man who humbled Samuel Durell!"

He shoved the half-filled glass toward Durell.

It was the moment he had been waiting for, one of those splinters of time that divide despair from hope, death from life.

Casually, he extended his right hand until it touched the bottom of the glass, then in a blur of motion rammed it back into the Corsican's face, not sparing his strength.

There came a thin crackling sound as the fragile vessel splintered and bright blood spurted where the jagged flinders had lodged in the man's lips and cheeks.

Cesari stumbled back screaming and the MAB barked. Durell felt the hot muzzle blast whiff past his head as he snatched his .38 from the table. He fired hurriedly and lunged through the door. He did not know if he had hit the Corsican, but there was no time to make sure.

He ran into a prostitute guiding a drunken Arab businessman to her crib and knocked them both down. They cursed him as he reeled, got his footing and plunged ahead. No one fired at him, but he heard shouts from behind. He glanced back, saw men swarm out of the back door of the bar after him. Durell vaulted a sheet metal fence and landed in a commotion of frightened chickens behind a house of dried mud and dung bricks.

He pushed through its back door. A woman screamed.

There came the heavy pad of bare feet as a man leaped toward him; something whished through the death-dark air and he ducked instinctively.

"I won't hurt you," he said as calmly as he could. "Let me out." He heard the renewed panic of the chickens —the men were coming into the house.

The blade flashed through the gloom again. Durell grabbed, found an arm, threw the man away. Then he flung himself through the front exit into the loud, stinking street a few doors down from the Melotti beer sign. Someone there saw him, called into the bar. The others were barging through the house behind him, the woman still screaming. The only way to go was up the street, away from the bar.

He started to run, then stopped, petrified for a second with shock. Automobile headlamps raced toward him. They were too close to evade. He hoisted the .38 and aimed through the blinding shine at the driver's side of the windshield.

At the same instant tires yelped and the car lurched to a halt.

"Cajun, baby! Get in!"

It was Mira, driving his BMW.

She drove the fine car brutally, flailing it around the corners, beating it into powerful surges on the straightaways; cursing it, Durell and fate, in Italian, Amharic, Arabian and several other languages.

"Calm down. Don't break your neck," Durell said.

"It's your neck I'd like to break, leaving me in that wrecked hotel room. Did you think I would wait for you there? Answer all the questions when the management brought the authorities? Believe me, I've seen enough of Ethiopian jails."

Durell imagined she had. "I figured you could take care of yourself," he said.

She took both hands off the wheel, gestured wildly. "So you just left me holding the bag!" she shouted. The BMW took a stomach-turning veer toward a stone building and she grabbed the wheel at the last moment. They debouched onto a wide avenue.

"Better slow down if you don't like jail," Durell said. "How did you find me?"

"I followed you. It wasn't hard with the sound of your gun. When I saw you enter the bar, I went and got your car. You left the keys in the room with your suitcoat. I had carried it away with me, because I was afraid it might contain something you'd rather not have fall into the wrong hands."

Again Durell was struck by her competence. "It seems that you're always picking up after me," he said. "Where are we headed?"

"My apartment."

"We can't go there. Not now. Tessema and Hennessey are using it. We mustn't bring any heat down on them."

"Are we being followed?" She glanced into the mirror.

"I don't think so, but we can't take chances."

"What, then? You'd be crazy to go back to the Ras."

"I've got to get to Gondar," Durell said. The clock was still running. He was lucky to be alive and aware of it. But as long as he was, every energy would be directed toward the mountains where the forces of madness cultivated their seeds of awesome destruction.

"Find another hotel," he said. "I'll leave you there. In the morning you can return to your shop."

"Oh, no. I'm getting out of this madhouse with you," she said. "Maybe I won't ever come back."

Durell had not wanted to take her and had not expected her to ask. Now that she had, he considered the merits of it. She knew the people and the country as only a native could. That would be helpful. He could leave her in Gondar when he went into the mountains.

"Are you sure you want to come?" he asked.

"You know it, Sam, baby."

She sought safety and every hour she spent with him would only increase her danger—but there was no time left to argue. "Head south," he said.

"I have already."

15

No cars were visible ahead or behind as they rushed through the countryside. Tossed hills and sleeping villages were splotched with paraffin whiteness in the shining night. Durell was reminded of the emptiness of this vast land, where hermits prayed out their lives and leopards roamed the valley forests.

Mira watched the road intently, her almond eyes narrowed, lips taut with concentration. "Have you got a cigarette, Sam?" she asked.

"Sorry, no. Are you nervous?"

"Just because someone tried to kill us? Oh, no." She laughed a little crazily. "How can you sit there so calmly? You like danger, don't you? I can see it in your eyes."

"You'd better relax," said Durell. "We've got a long way to go and you're going to wear yourself out, if you don't."

Briefly he considered the drive ahead. They would cross the Gash River out of ELF-troubled Eritrea into Tigre Province; wind on through forlorn Aksum, capital of the Queen of Sheba a thousand years before Christ; and bridge the Tekeze into Begemdir Province. Sometime in the morning they would arrive in Gondar, a town of seventeenth-century castles near Lake Tana, source of the Blue Nile. He would meet Hennessey in a safe house there tomorrow afternoon.

"What happened back there, after you ran out of the hotel?" Mira asked.

"A man named Joseph Cesari was waiting for me with a gun." The car suddenly swerved. "Hey, I said relax," Durell said.

"There was an animal, something in the road."

"What do you know about Cesari?"

"Nothing." Mira shrugged her small shoulders. "I never heard of him. Did you—did you have to . . . ?"

"Kill him? I tried. It was very confused after that. If I succeeded it won't stop them. I think we're up against a big organization with lots of money behind it." He heard the heightened whine of the engine as Mira pressed harder on the accelerator. She glanced at the rear-vision mirror. There seemed no honesty in trying to reassure her, Durell thought. The others would guess that his next logical move was toward the mountains, and there was only one road from Ahmara to Gondar. He had penetrated their outer defenses, was taking the battle onto their home ground.

They must react to that swiftly and with all of their might. That is what Cesari, their professional, would tell them, if he still lived.

Durell did not underrate the Corsican. Next time he would be cautious and even more deadly. He would be shooting not only for hire, but for revenge—a vendetta to cleanse his reputation of the humiliation Durell had caused him.

"Cesari and his men almost got Tessema at the airstrip. Somebody must have told him Hennessey was going there," he said.

"It could have been coincidence." Mira did not take her eyes from the road. A cow's-skull scarecrow flashed in and out of the radiance of headlamps, off to one side of the highway. Southward, where the road led them toward Adi Ugri, hills bunched and roughed into mountains, moonlight broke against flat-topped *ambas.*

Durell said: "I don't know about the monarchist plot to take over the country, Mira. They could be working with Cesari's outfit. You and Ineyu have been pretty cozy with them. Maybe you've been keeping them informed—maybe they passed the word along to Cesari."

Abruptly she punched the brakes and whipped the car to a halt on the shoulder of the road. She glared at him and said, "I don't think I like you very much, Sam, baby."

"Look, I'm just lucky that someone isn't putting pieces of me in a litter bag right now. I don't like that very much, either." He saw Mira's eyes roll toward her purse, between the bucket seats. She had no hope of beating him to the little .32 nesting there, and she did not try.

Durell said: "Deste Giroud saved my life at the Villa d'Este. She turned me over to Nadu Ambaw. I learned how you and Ineyu had been collaborating with them, supplying them with funds. It's senseless to deny it."

"Let me tell you about that, Sam . . ."

"Go ahead." Durell kept his hand away from the snubnosed pistol in his waistband. He had no reason to frighten her further; he would not need the gun in any case.

Mira seemed to compose her thoughts as they sat in the still vastness. A car broke the solitude, going in the opposite direction. The torn air of its passage settled and the only sounds were the muttering of the idling BMW, the whisper of its heater.

Then Mira said: "Sure, I passed money along. I just ran errands for Ineyu, and he told me to. In our business, you do what you're told and no questions, right? But I assumed the money came from K Section, that it was authorized for the purpose. Was I wrong?"

"I don't know."

"It wouldn't have surprised me if the order came straight from Sugar Cube—after all, the U.S. was on very friendly terms with the monarchy. Things haven't gone so well since the military came to power."

"And you told them nothing about me?"

"Not a word, I swear it. Well, do we go on or not?" Her voice was challenging. "Am I supposed to step outside and get a bullet through the head? I know what men like you are capable of. You'd sacrifice me and a hundred like me to win the smallest advantage. You're remorseless."

"I can't let emotion distract me, if that's what you mean," Durell said in a level voice. He regarded her in the dim light of the dash, the highland breeze whimpering against the car. Her glowing eyes went flat and the color drained from her cheeks as he took the .32 revolver from her handbag. He emptied the cartridges from its chamber and dropped them into his left coat pocket, where they would not mix with the .38s in the right, then returned the gun and snapped the handbag shut.

She was only a beautiful, sweet-scented woman. Somehow his senses, all of his finely-honed intuition, could probe no more deeply than that, he thought with regret.

"Let's move on," he said.

Relief loosened Mira's face as she put the car in gear and pulled back onto the macadam.

It was almost one o'clock when they passed through Adi Ugri, a typical roadside town of dirty, ramshackle dwellings. Things were going as well as could be expected now, Durell reflected. They were making good time. He watched the miles ripple past, aware of the lifting landscape, terraces of millet and teff, the sudden hush of road sounds as an abyss surprised their passage.

"Sam?"

He realized the car was slowing and looked up. Someone in the middle of the road swung a flashlight, signaling them to halt.

"Should I stop?" Mira asked uncertainly.

"You'd better; it looks like soldiers." Beyond the circling point of light, the moon revealed a long line of vehicles, the movement of scores of men.

Mira halted the car on the blacktop and a corporal in combat dress bent to their window. A rifle was slung across his back. The beam of his torch burst against their faces. "The road is closed," he said in Amharic.

"For how long?" Durell asked.

He shrugged his shoulders. "I am sorry, sir. You must go back the way you came."

94

"Will it be an hour? Two hours? Three?" Durell struggled to keep a rein on his impatience.

"Maybe longer, sir. I have orders to send southbound traffic back to Adi Ugri."

"We passed through there an hour ago!" Mira said.

"It is regrettable." The corporal put on a sorrowful face.

Beyond the corporal the road was busy with milling troops, shouting officers, supply trucks. Clearly preparations were underway for an attack against a nearby enemy.

Mira's eyes questioned Durell by the light of the dash. "Turn around," he said. She did as she was told, and he said: "Drive slowly. A dirt road turns off to the left about a mile back. We'll take that."

"Without knowing where it leads?"

"Maybe it loops through a village and comes back to the highway beyond the army roadblock." Durell watched for the turnoff.

"What if the army catches us? I don't want to face a firing squad."

Durell pointed. "There's the road. Kill the lights. I'll take the wheel."

Mira's small foot lifted from the gas pedal, and the car drifted to a halt on the shoulder of the highway. She made no effort to turn onto the narrow wagon track. "Sam, let's do what the man said and go back to Adi Ugri. Please."

"That would waste hours, Mira. I said kill the lights." He glanced over his shoulder. There was nothing to indicate they still were in view of the troops, but he was taking no chances.

Her fingers touched the light switch reluctantly. "If we do get caught, they'll be harder on me than on you."

Durell remembered her dossier. "Because you have a police record?"

"K Section doesn't miss much, does it?" Mira eyed him sharply. "I've had to do lots of things to get ahead that I'd rather not have done; I may do more yet," she said with defiance.

Durell forced an impatient breath through his nostrils and yanked the keys from the ignition—there was no point in giving her an opportunity to drive off without him—then slid out his door and strode around the car to the driver's side. "Move over; I can't spare any more time," he said.

She hesitated, glaring at him, and he shoved her roughly with his hip to get her out of the way.

The rutted track was easy to follow in the shining night, even without headlights. They wound into a defile cleaving a low ridge and crossed a dry stream bed, stones chuckling beneath the tires. Durell judged that the troops were using the ridge to screen their arrangements, and that they would sweep in this direction, probably at dawn, perhaps earlier. He just hoped he would be past the danger zone before they struck.

Mira sat against the far door, rigid with anger and apprehension. Her legs were stiff, as if she would push the floor out of the car. The BMW bounced, lurched and wobbled although Durell drove very slowly. Beyond the windows boulders and stands of eucalyptus wore snowy caps of moonlight.

Then they rounded a curve and a premonition of disaster licked coldly at the back of Durell's neck.

Pale metallic flickers of moonlight glinted in the mangled shadows dead ahead.

Rifle barrels.

16

Durell jammed the gearshift lever into reverse and floored the accelerator. The force of the reversal hurled Mira toward the windshield; she braced herself, hands against the dash. He lessened the pressure on the gas pedal; he could see almost nothing through the rear window, but at least they had regained the shelter of boulders embraced by the curve.

"You saw the men?" he asked as he fought to keep the car on the trail.

"Two," she said.

"No, three for sure."

The BMW emitted a screech of torn metal as it side-swiped a face of stone, and something yanked the wheel from his grasp. They caromed out of the cart ruts and the car's rear crunched into a steep slope of loose gravel. There was no place here to turn around and no time to find one. Durell was out of the door before the car had stopped rocking, the smell of dust and dew strong in his nostrils, his grip relaxed and ready about his .38.

"Get out. Quickly." His voice was low, urgent.

The bloated moon showed Mira's frightened face. Her hands jerked at the door handle, but the door was jammed. She gasped with the effort.

The pad of running feet came from around the bend.

Durell bent through his door and dragged Mira out of the car. She started to run up the trail toward the highway, but he caught her, spun her half-around. "This way," he said, and they ran for jumbled shadows in the silvery landscape. Fragments of Amharic resonated in the chill, clear air. Durell sensed the impact of bullets that did not come. Then he was in a cleft in the ridge, shielded from the moonlight, waiting.

Something scurried away, a fox, perhaps, or a small mountain cat. Durell's breath came in light puffs; Mira gasped for air and moved closer to him. He rose to his knees and watched as three dim figures rushed around the curve, caught sight of the car and stopped, weapons raised. Flash suppressors and bulky magazine clips on the rifles indicated that they were modern and capable of automatic fire. Two of the men wore calf-length coats girded about with belts and bandoliers; the third had a shaggy animal pelt thrown over his shoulders.

There came the call of a nightbird, the mocking laughter of a hyena.

"They're not soldiers," Mira whispered.

"Maybe ELF," Durell replied. He kept his eyes on them as they cautiously peered through the doors and windows of the car.

"Or *shifta* bandits; I wish you had left my gun loaded."

"You'd only get yourself killed. We can't shoot it out; they've got us outgunned."

"I'd feel better with a weapon."

Her hand slipped into his grasp. It was trembling and cold. She was a small shadow beside him, vulnerable as those painted by the westering moon. He regretted her dependency; he could not allow it to impede him or endanger his mission.

Mira suddenly dug the little .32 out of her purse. "Give me the bullets for my gun," she said.

"No."

"You still think I'd use it on you."

"Why should I chance it?"

"I wish I had stayed in Asmara."

"You insisted on coming."

She sat stiffly, arms folded beneath her breasts.

The three men formed a huddle by the BMW's front bumper. They made no effort to keep their voices down and seemed to be arguing a course of action, but Durell could make little of the snatches he heard. Mira's ear was more attuned to the language. "Can you catch what they are saying?" he whispered.

"They're sending for more men."

At that moment one trotted out of sight behind the bend.

Durell felt sweat around his collar.

A breeze moved stems of dry grass, bringing the smells of woodsmoke and grainfields, as Durell regarded the two men remaining at the car. He had hoped they would come after him so that he could make a circle and beat them back to the BMW. Now he thought about moving further away, along the base of the ridge, but rejected the idea. That was what they expected him to do, to run as hard as he could.

"Come on," he said. He hurried away, staying in the shadows and using the lay of the ground for concealment.

In a little while Mira said, "This isn't the way back to the highway.

"We're going the way the runner went, paralleling the trail," Durell said.

"That will take us right to them!" Mira's hand went to her throat. "What if they are bandits?"

Durell said nothing and kept moving.

"If they are ELF, they'll kill us or hold us for ransom."

"The laugh would be on them—no one would claim us." Durell's tread was light, his tall frame bent slightly forward. Mira stumbled and made a small, compressed sound of discomfort. He motioned for her to stop, cocked an ear toward the road. There came a confused bustling of feet, the muted jangle of fighting gear. "Don't talk. Don't move. They're coming," he said.

He flattened himself in the brittle grass, the odor of sunburnt humus close to his nose, and willed the men to pass without taking alarm. They numbered about a dozen, moving rapidly in the direction of the car. Moon sparks flashed from their bandoliers and weapons, and Durell, even closer to the road here than he'd been back at the car, saw their grim, dark faces clearly. They carried a hodgepodge of arms, but most appeared to be equipped with Belgian-made FAL automatic rifles. They were not likely to be ELF, who depended primarily on Soviet weapons smuggled in by Arab states.

When they had passed, Durell waited another minute, wary of stragglers. Mira was shivering, either from fear or the cold. He took his passport and the pistol cartridges from his coat and put it over her shoulders. The chill breeze fussed in the grass and pressed through his thin shirt. A dog barked in the near distance.

"Let's go," he whispered, and tugged on her hand.

She balked, nodding in the direction from which the men had come. "I'm not going that way," she said.

"They won't expect us to; it's our best bet. They will find you up here."

"What about the car? We can't go far without it." Mira rubbed a sore ankle.

"I'm counting on the army's attack to draw them away from it. Then maybe we can get back to it in the confusion. At worst we should be able to turn ourselves over to the military."

Mira pulled the jacket closer about her and scanned the grotesque disorder of boulders and gullies. "Can't we go to the military now?"

"They must be a couple of miles away; it's too risky. I thought you were afraid of the authorities."

"Not as afraid as I am of those others," she said in a thick voice.

Gunfire sounded from the defile behind them. Mira grasped Durell's arm; the points of her manicured nails gouged his flesh. "They're shooting at shadows," he said.

He headed down the slope.

Mira came after him.

About three minutes passed, then they came to fields of millet that spread across the wide floor of a valley. Their legs made rushing sounds as they moved through the grain toward the blotted outlines of a village a few hundred yards below. Low mountains thrust up all around, their ridges standing out harshly. A blank-walled monastery crested a nearby cliff of basalt. The demented laughter of hyenas bounced from mountainside to mountainside. Durell heard a throaty cough and wondered if a leopard hunted geleda baboon down there in a nearby ravine.

He glanced back at the ridge, where the search party would be turning over rocks looking for them, and urged Mira on.

The irregular wall of shadow before them resolved itself into huts and trees. The cone-shaped thatch roof of a country church rose above the village, an eight-armed cross at its peak. Durell scanned the fields, then the *tukuls* clustered beyond a long, low wall of loosely piled stones. He saw the frosty gleam of trucks and cars parked a hundred yards to the right, slightly downhill, and his eyes traced the dirt road from the ridge and across the valley where it twisted out of sight. Horses were tethered near the vehicles.

The only other sign of habitation was thin smoke curling through thatched roofs.

Sentinels doubtlessly were posted among the mound-shaped huts, but they were concealed from his view. He and Mira lay in a shallow draw a few yards from the village, their bodies flattening mattresses of brittle millet stalks; Durell did not relish giving up its shelter to reach the wall. A scant twenty yards away was an opening in the stone fence. He felt certain a guard was near it.

"Those vehicles down there can't belong to the people who live here, can they?" he asked.

"They couldn't afford them—they live hand to mouth," Mira replied.

"Then the men we have to worry about must have quartered themselves on the villagers. What are our chances of getting help in there?"

"You're not going into the village, are you?"

"I don't want to be out here when the sun comes up; we'll be seen for sure." Durell's eyes made a circuit of the field, where air currents pushed quicksilver ripples across the grain. His gaze returned to the *tukuls* as something moved beyond the wall. It was the merest flicker of a moonbeam, the smudge of a shadow. He remained motionless, eyes narrowing, and made out the dappled shape of a man. It was the sentry he had been looking for. The man was back among the kosso trees, a comfortable distance from the opening in the stone fence, rifle slung carelessly over his shoulder.

"Listen!" Mira said.

Durell placed his hand on her shoulder, feeling a cadaveric rigidity there as she tensed with fright. A man was yelling; another joined in and the noise grew to a chorus of shouts. Durell twisted his head in the direction of the sounds and saw the men emerge from the shadow of the ridge and charge into the millet.

They were coming straight toward him.

They followed the dark path of trodden grain he and Mira had made across the field.

"We've got to get into the village," Durell said.

"No!" Mira cried under her breath. There was a touch of rage in her voice.

"There's no other choice. Stay close to me."

Durell crawled to a narrow strip of raw earth that separated the field from the entrance to the village. The commotion had drawn the guard to the wall fifteen or twenty paces to the right. The others ran and stumbled over the uneven ground, fell and picked themselves up. They could not see Durell and Mira yet, but gained on

101

them swiftly. Behind a thin screen of straw Durell hesitated a fraction, then darted through the wall into the deeper night of the kosso trees. He concealed himself behind a tree trunk, pressing his shoulder against the rough bark, and glanced from the guard to the field as he waited for Mira.

She was frightened, but he knew she would not panic; she had a steel-hard streak of will that had carried her through as bad as this before.

Somewhere a goat bleated. The barnyard odor of the village mingled with the fragrance of lamplike kosso blossoms prized by the raw-meat-eating Ethiopians as an antidote for tapeworm.

It seemed that Mira would never come. Then she was there beside him, her purse swinging daintily from her arm.

Durell turned to move deeper into the village, saw movement out of the corner of his eye and froze.

The guard must have heard Mira.

He strode toward them, hooked his thumb under the sling of his automatic rifle to bring the weapon off his shoulder. Durell couldn't give him time to complete the motion, or he and Mira would be as good as dead. His leaping rush was a blur, over almost the second it began, and the butt of his .38 crashed into the man's skull just behind the ear. The rifle slid away, clattering noisly to the hard-packed earth, but there was no help for it; the sentry's legs buckled as if scythed, and Durell caught him under the arms and dragged him into the darkness beneath the trees.

The man wore a Christian neck cord, fifty or sixty dark blue beads on a string to keep Satan at least forty paces distant.

Durell hoped the charm worked.

The sentry was dead.

17

They ran through a twisted confusion of

lanes and footpaths toward the center of the village. Shouts came from behind as Durell veered to the left, slowed to a trot and kept in the shadows beside the black walls of *tukuls*. He did not think they had seen him. Mira's presence was a touch at his back, the whisper of her breath.

The alarm was spreading, the sound of running feet all around. Durell saw shadowy forms rush past a crossing ahead, then nothing.

He stopped before a plank door: "In here."

"Not me, Sam, baby: I'm going that way." Her finger jabbed toward a rafter-thin space between the huts. A dust of sweat gleamed above her lips.

It was a large village, and many of the foe had taken to the streets. The odds were that only legitimate residents were on the other side of the door. Durell spread his hand across the narrow width of her back, pushed the door open, shoved her inside. A dozen pairs of eyes, their whites oily in the glow from the firehole, returned his stare. He pushed the door closed with his heel, his .38 held before him with easy competence.

"My god, it stinks in here." Mira made a face and backed against a wall plastered with mixed mud, ash and manure.

The air was raw with smoke that wafted up beside the centerpole, adding to layers of soot that covered the thatch. Near the firehole lay a grinding stone, grains of millet scattered on it. A few cooking utensils and some clothing hung from hooks on the wall. Through a flimsy partition Durell glimpsed the great eyes of an ox sheltered here during the night from wild animals.

He briefly studied the dark faces: there were an elderly man probably withered beyond his years by toil and disease, skin tight and shining over fleshless cheekbones; three younger men, short and sturdy; several shy women and numbers of children, including an infant feeding at its mother's breast with tugs and smacking.

Three of the men at on pillboxlike stools of woven straw; the others huddled on skin-covered ridges of earth that served as beds.

No one moved.

They watched him and the gun.

"Our luck's holding! they look like villagers," Durell said.

"Don't trust them." Mira said.

Durell spoke to the peasants. "We came to ask help and to offer it; we won't harm you," he said in Amharic. "Who are the men who have taken over your village?"

The eyes of the others turned to the old man and he replied in the liquid tongue: bands of men had arrived throughout the previous day and into the night. They had taken the homes of the villagers, saying they would sleep there and leave in the morning. "Where they came from and where they go, I do not know. In the meantime, we are crowded together like goats."

"Are they ELF?" Mira asked impatiently.

The man shook his head and kept his eyes on Durell's revolver. "They revealed nothing to us," he said.

"He could be lying," Mira said.

"I doubt they are ELF," Durell said. "It's predominately Moslem, and that guard was a Christian. Bandits always hit and run, so I'd rule them out as well."

He turned again to the old man. "Do they have a female with them—a small, foreign-looking woman with golden hair?"

The man's eyes brightened and he nodded.

Mira gave Durell a puzzled stare. "How did you know that?" she asked.

"Deste Giroud," he said. "Monarchists are holding the village, gathering to move into the mountains south of here." He paused, hearing the men who hunted him kick in a door somewhere out there. Strident voices mingled with cries of fear. Then he said: "We've stumbled into Nadu Ambaw's encampment."

"You're crazy! Deste and Ambaw are in Asmara!"

"They're here. Ambaw said he was going into the mountains tonight. Deste begged to come with him. He was under surveillance—the army must have been waiting for an opportunity like this, a chance to bag him along with his lieutenants."

The villagers looked uncomprehendingly from Durell to Mira. Their eyes jerked with fright as another door crashed in and the search went on. It was coming closer.

Mira said: "*Dejasmatch* Ambaw wouldn't harm me; he thinks I'm on his side."

"Deste convinced him I was his enemy."

"Maybe if we talked to him . . ."

"Too late; he tried to kill me; too much violence has been done."

"Then let me go by myself. I will talk to him."

"No."

"If his men find us, they may kill us both! Why should I pay for your problems?" She came for the door. Durell tossed her away and hardly felt the effort.

She rose from the dirt floor and anger pinched the skin at the corners of her dark eyes. She spoke slowly, controlling her fury. "If we get through this alive, I'll find a way to pay you back," she cried.

"So be it. We understand each other."

Sounds of the hunt came from all over the village—it was only a matter of time before the men would burst in here. Durell turned his attention to the peasants, and said:

"I can help you, but you must help me. Send someone to tell the golden-haired woman to meet Mira Seragate in the church—Mira Seragate. You understand?"

The elder spoke to a man who sat beside him: "Do as he says. Go quickly."

The man pulled a goatskin over his shoulders and approached the door. Durell stepped to the right and motioned with his pistol for the man to go out. The man pushed the door open slightly and bent to the crack as if scenting the air. Then the door scraped against dry earth and he was gone.

Mira said, "What makes you think Deste will come without telling *Dejasmatch* Ambaw?"

"You are friends; she'll find out what's up before going to him, I suspect. Our best hope is to use her to get out of the area."

Durell turned back to the villagers. "The army is camped nearby and will attack your village at any moment," he said. "Many of your people may be killed or injured, unless they evacuate their homes immediately. When your man returns, go warn your friends and run for the shelter of the hills."

There was a moment of shocked silence. By the light of the firehole, Durell saw eyes widen and lips part and women pull their children close instinctively. Then all eyes turned to the old man, and he uttered brief verbs of command, and the people crowded around the door. He touched the ground with his right hand and brought his fingers to his lips, then placed them on Durell's shoulder. His face grave, he opened the door and stepped out of the way of the others. "*Hid! Hid!* Go! Go!" he said, and his charges flocked into the night. He followed on their heels, not looking back.

They weren't waiting for the return of the messenger.

"Looks as if word of the army's methods has preceded it," Durell said.

There was pandemonium in the village as Durell and Mira slipped outside. Villagers pounded on doors to awaken their neighbors; men, women and children ran among the huts; families became separated, husbands calling to wives and wives to their fledglings. Caught unaware, Ambaw's disorganized troops challenged and were ignored; grappled and were overwhelmed; fired shots into the air and only added to the hysteria.

It was not difficult to move anonymously through the swirling humanity.

Somewhere on the stony path to the church, Mira vanished.

Durell did not pause to search for her. He wondered if she would betray him to Ambaw and decided she might, to save her own skin.

Suddenly a clump of cedars intervened before the church. Durell plunged through them and the branches

106

slapped at his skin and clothing. He came out in front of the Coptic place of worship. Its shaggy, cone-shaped roof loomed over him, a straw effigy of the stark, moon-clad mountains beyond.

Durell ran across a courtyard, lunged through an open doorway and found himself in darkness that was as absolute as the void before creation. There seemed to be no pews or chairs. He felt through the emptiness stiff-legged, like a blind man. A wall touched his fingers; another doorway was just to the left. He remembered that these churches were built in three concentric circles, an exit at each cardinal point of the compass. He went into the *kudist*, the second circle.

The noise from outside penetrated the thatch of the roof; tiny stars of moonglow dotted the darkness up there.

Durell's pistol grip felt wet in his hand; a fragrance of incense touched his nose. From high up came the squeak of bats.

He waited, kneeling on one knee, his gun ready. He cast his eyes back and forth, not knowing whether to expect Deste or a murderous Ambaw.

Then an explosion wracked the village. There came a second blast and a third in rapid succession.

Mortars.

Sprigs of thatch sifted down from the roof. Screams and confused shouts mixed with the deadly rattle of gunfire. The attack had begun, triggered prematurely, perhaps, by the tumult in the village.

Durell heard the vehicles parked nearby grind to life. He made no move as a minute passed, then another.

"Mira?"

His eyes turned toward the small sound in the dark.

The voice was Deste's.

"Here," Durell called over the bedlam.

Quickly he took four silent steps along the wall. The precaution had been unnecessary; she did not fire at the sound of his voice. He could neither see not hear her move, but he sensed that she came toward where he had spoken. He watched the flat blackness and hoped to catch a glint of metal if she carried a gun or knife.

"Who are you? Where's Mira?" Her words were touched with urgency.

Durell heard a muffled noise of movement close by. It was the only beacon he needed as he lunged, made a wide sweep with his arms and gathered the unbelievably light bundle of her body, pinning her against his chest.

"Who do you think it is?" His tone was harsh.

"Sam? Sam Durell! Wait . . ."

Her breath burst against his face as he crushed her. She struggled violently, hooked a leg behind his knee and they rolled in the dust. Durell increased the pressure—a bit tighter and her spine would snap. Suddenly she went limp.

He did not loosen his hold.

"Please . . ." It was barely audible.

Another salvo of mortar rounds shook the earth, blast waves ripping thatch loose from above.

Durell pressed the muzzle of his .38 into the soft flesh under Deste's chin, searched her quickly and thoroughly. She was unarmed. He sat back and kept the gun against her neck. He could not see her face, but her pewter eyes shone dimly.

"What are you doing here?" she asked. "Is Mira with you?"

"It's a long story; Mira's on her own now."

"And you're going to repay me for Asmara? Listen, Sam . . ."

"I can't afford to settle old debts now, maybe later—you're going to get me out of here."

"I'll help you, Sam. You can trust me."

"Don't ask the impossible. Where's Ambaw?"

"He and the other leaders have left for the mountains."

Durell kept his gun on Deste as he considered the situation. The racket of a full-fledged firefight raged around the village. Ambaw must have left a rear guard to delay pursuit, he decided. "Let's go," he said.

He followed her to an outer doorway, his pistol at her back. The sullen flicker of burning thatch swarmed on the doorsill. Orange wisps of dry, stinging smoke trailed across the little courtyard, and there was an iron stench left by the high-explosive mortar rounds.

"Mitiku? Ato?" Deste called.

Durell ducked back into the shadows. Splintering noises of the fires mingled with the moan of stray bullets. Two faces peered inside.

"They will help us," Deste said.

"Why?"

"They are friends of my mother's family."

"Not good enough."

"I have paid them well."

"I trust that more than old family ties," Durell said. By the fiery light of the courtyard he saw that Mitiku and Ato carried new FAL rifles like those of the men who had pursued him and Mira. Apparently the monarchists had purchased modern weapons, but hoped to keep them hidden from police surveillance. He remembered the old Mausers so conspicuous on the guards at Ambaw's villa. He shoved his pistol against Deste's back and said, "Tell them to sling the rifles and keep their hands away from them. They're to stay in front of us."

Deste repeated the order in Amharic; the men did as they were told, their eyes questioning her.

"Now, go!" Durell said.

They darted across the empty courtyard, Durell in the rear, and bent into a pathway that cut sharply to the left, away from the stutter of combat. Most of the fighting was to the north and west of them, and they encountered no one as they hurried out of the village. The moon was only a finger above a western peak; dawn would come soon. Durell glanced back at the wavering orange pall of smoke rising from the burning *tukuls*.

Gunfire broke out on their left, somewhere just beyond the verge of a gleaming field of millet.

"You know the way through Ambaw's sentries? Some may have got cut off up here," Durell said.

"Of course. I wish you would put that pistol away," Deste said.

"I should use it on you for turning me over to Ambaw in Asmara."

"I'm helping you now."

"It had better not be the same way."

Mitiku halted, spoke under his breath to Ato. Ato

109

nodded his shining, close-cropped head, and Durell saw the glimmer of a golden earring by his wiry neck.

"You go alone from here, lord," Mitiku said.

Durell looked down from the lip of a dry, treeless gully, scarred into the edge of the valley by the *kiremt*, the big rains blown in seasonally from the Indian Ocean. It was a black crayon mark scrawled toward the indistinct line of an abyss maybe half a mile southward.

Deste said, "Don't get lost in there. A little way down is a pond where the villagers water their animals. A path goes up the other side from there. It will take you back to the highway."

Durell moved around the trio crabwise, his gun covering them at point-blank range. "Turn around and get out of here," he said.

The two men looked uncertainly at Deste, weapons still slung. The waves of her long hair shone like ribbons of gold. She looked truly regal, Durell thought.

"I regret . . ." she began.

"No speeches—be glad you're alive."

She turned on her heel, and he watched her and Mitiku and Ato until they disappeared over a rise in the fields.

Feet slipping a bit in the loose earth, Durell descended the sharply inclined side of the gully. A large animal ran across the path and up the other slope. The moon was gone. He noticed there was no longer any sound from the village, no firing, no shouts.

He wondered about Mira's fate. She made an interesting contrast to Deste, he thought: beautiful, yet so different. Deste, utterly self-contained, with a past that must have provided her with almost anything she had desired; Mira, mercurial, uncertain and grasping, because life had started her with so little.

The pond lay before him like polished iron in the gray, pre-dawn light.

He skirted the pond, found the clay path Deste had mentioned and scrambled toward the top of the eroded gully wall. The tropical sunrise changed the sky second by second in a slow-motion explosion of color. Birds chirped and twittered. To the south a column of vultures twisted slowly.

Coming over the top, Durell saw that soldiers were everywhere, loose groups of squads and platoons that shuffled toward the highway. He had hoped to avoid the military, but now that was impossible. He was certain to be challenged and would need a pass. The most effective course, he decided, was to present himself as an innocent bystander with nothing to hide.

He loosened his grip on the pistol hanging by his thigh and it fell into the grass beside the path.

A steel-helmeted captain and two troopers were approaching him. Durell waved, gave them a weary smile. It did not abate the suspicion in their eyes. He took his passport from his hip pocket and gave it to the officer. "I'm glad I found you; it's been a long night," he said in Amharic. "May I speak with your commanding officer?"

The captain looked through the passport, then stared at Durell with unveiled curiosity. "You will come with me, please," he said courteously.

They escorted him to a place beside the Gondar highway, where about twenty trucks and scout cars were parked. The captain entered the command post, a khaki-colored tent with an awning in front, and returned to tell Durell there would be a short wait.

Durell sat down on the stiff grass. As the minutes passed, he drew his knees up and wrapped his arms around his legs. Impatience surrendered to fatigue, and his head drooped forward and he dozed.

Something tapped his shoulder. His face jerked up. The sun was hot on the back of his neck. A soldier motioned for him to follow, and he got stiffly to his feet. Then he realized with astonishment that his coat was over his shoulders. He supposed Mira had put it there while he slept—the soldiers must have found her and then released her, but where had she gone? He saw no sign of her.

He glanced at his wristwatch: it was almost eight o'clock. The "short wait" had stretched to nearly two hours.

He was showed into the command post, where a field

111

communications rig crackled at a radio operator with bloodshot eyes.

The sight of the other man in the tent jolted him—he recognized from K Section file photos the cunning eyes and foxlike face of Colonel Mamo Tekle, and he foresaw trouble. Tekle was chief of the army's newly formed Special Branch, an agency so confidential that the government had never acknowledged its existence. Ineyu had reported that it functioned as an elite secret police, and that Tekle was clever, cruel and of unquestioned loyalty to the regime.

The colonel was dressed in heavily starched fatigues and sat beside a folding table. On the table were Durell's green passport and a riding crop of rhinoceros hide, nothing else. Dark spots on the riding crop might have been dried blood. Teckle clenched his riding crop and spoke curtly in English, a man with too many things to do. "Sit down, Mr. Durell; it was sensible of you to come to us voluntarily."

"I need a pass, otherwise I wouldn't have troubled you," Durell said matter-of-factly.

"Oh? A pass?"

Durell did not care for his tone. "To get through your zone of operations."

"Where do you wish to go? Are you in a hurry?"

"Gondar. No rush." Durell wondered how long this would take, and impatience chewed on him. If he failed to meet Hennessey in Gondar as planned, Hennessey would proceed alone.

Tekle's face hardened. "What were you doing with the monarchist dogs?" he said.

"They stopped my car; I didn't know who they were."

Long seconds passed as Tekle made a show of examining Durell's passport. Quietly, he said: "You do an extraordinary amount of traveling, I see by your documents. Why did you come to Ethiopia, Mr. Durell?"

"I'm merely a tourist, sir—I suggest you radio the American embassy for confirmation of my status."

The colonel's mouth smiled, but there was no humor in his eyes. "That will not be necessary," he said.

"Then may I have a pass?"

Tekle seemed to be thinking about something else and stared through Durell with dark, vague eyes.

"You would not wish to detain an American citizen without just cause," Durell said.

Tekle's eyes focused on him again. "Of course not," he said. "You will need a pass. The monarchists have received modern weapons from Europe; someone is smuggling them into the country. We believe the gunrunners to be Westerners. Yesterday a tall Westerner like you, but in native dress, was seen at the villa of Nadu Ambaw, the leader of the monarchists. He subsequently eluded our police in Asmara. I tell you that so that you can conduct yourself accordingly and remain above suspicion."

Durell saw that Tekle watched closely for his reaction. He kept his face bland and said, "I'll try to do that, sir."

Tekle signed a form and handed it to Durell. "You may go."

Durell picked up his passport and walked into the sunlight. It had gone easier than he'd expected, but he did not believe in miracles, and he was not relieved. He concluded that the secret police knew he was the man seen at Ambaw's—and that he would have Tekle to contend with again.

He walked half a mile along the highway, until he was out of sight of the troops, then swung away across fields and between rugged basaltic outcroppings to the place where the BMW had been parked.

It was gone.

He cursed softly and dug into his coat pocket. The keys were missing. Mira must have left without him.

His fingers found something else in the pocket, and he withdrew it and looked at it, standing in the hot, yellow glare of morning. It was the pink insole of Mira's slipper. On it she had hurriedly scrawled:

Ineyu. Degas Island. Lake Tana, 5 p.m.

It took Durell half an hour to skirt the military encampment and get back to the gully and find his pistol. Then it was another half hour before he reached the highway, and about forty-five minutes more until a car came along.

113

He stepped into the road, aimed the .38 at the windshield and the Volkswagen stopped. When he yanked the door open and told the nattily dressed young driver, "Take me to Gondar," he was in no mood for argument.

Ineyu was waiting for him.

And in the mountains the madmen who could blow up the world were waiting for no one.

18

After a while the fright went out of the driver's eyes and he became accustomed to the pistol on Durell's lap. They traveled silently, pausing only in Aksum to exchange rationing stamps for gasoline. When the sun was high and burning on the small car, the man indicated he wished to stop in Debarek to eat. Despite a ravenous hunger, Durell vetoed that. They continued on down the Walkefit Pass, where eucalyptus planted by the Italians canopied the twisting road and gelada baboons bounded down the slopes. Below Durell saw checkerboard fields of barley and rape on rolling hills splotched with the dark green of remnant forests. They were all that was left of once vast timber resources consumed heedlessly as centuries of emperors and feudal lords moved their entourages from place to place.

The Italians were only the last of many who had fought over this mysterious land, Durell remembered. Before them had come Arabs and Turks, spreading Islam; Portugese defending Christendom; Egyptians seeking control of the source of the Blue Nile, a river on which their lives depended and which the old Ethiopian kings threatened from time to time to poison.

Always in the end the land had returned to the dark bosom of the Ethiopians themselevs.

Gondar was a sea of tin roofs and eucalyptus trees, dotted with stone churches and castles left behind by nine kings. Two swift rivers kept its cradle green among the foothills. Youngsters played *gebeta* with beans, using holes carved into the sidewalk. Dark, willowy Ethiopian women in both western and ethnic dress haggled in the market stalls, along with tribal-scarred blacks from deep southern valleys, saried Indians, veiled Moslems and the ever-present sprinkling of Italians.

They passed the flowery gardens of the Iteghie Menen Hotel and drove around the parade ground in front of King Fasilidas's three-hundred-year-old castle onto the wide piazza. The Fascists had made Gondar their capital during the brief occupation, and at the far end of the piazza loomed the huge post office they had built, now shabby, its broken windows unreplaced under Ethiopian administration.

Even on the piazza, chauffer-driven limousines competed with basket-laden donkeys, herds of goats, strings of camels. Off the main street rocky alleys lined with ramshackle, mud-walled huts buzzed with flies and stank of animal and human dung.

Durell ordered the driver to pull over and got out near the Cinema Bar. Durell handed the driver the equivalent of about forty American dollars. The young man peered at it and then at Durell without expression.

"Thanks; I'm sorry," Durell said, and walked away. When he glanced back, the car still sat there with its motor running. Durell hoped the man had intended to come all the way to Gondar in the first place. Maybe the money would keep him from going to the police, at any rate.

He struck off on the first side street, then turned and paralleled the piazza back toward Fasilidas's castle. He looked at his watch: it was almost two o'clock. He would have only a brief time to go over the material Hennessey was to have brought. Then they would head for Lake Tana, about seventy kilometers south, to pick up Ineyu.

Durell considered Mira's message once more. If she had received the information through Colonel Tekle, it meant that she and Ineyu had some connection with Ethiopian officialdom. It had been natural enough for Ineyu to contact her instead of him—he'd had no way of knowing that Durell was in the country. If only Ineyu had not used military channels for the message, Durell would have felt no qualms.

As it was, however, he was alarmed at what appeared to be the Ethiopian Central's tangled web of allegiances to the U.S., the central regime, and even its monarchist opponents.

Ragged street urchins chattered around Durell like sparrows descending on spilled grain; adults stared as he passed the open doors of their houses. A Citroen van creaked by and chickens scattered. The walk had turned uphill now and sweat trickled down Durell's neck and the high, tormenting sun bathed him in fire. He kept his coat buttoned over the pistol in his waistband.

Then the somber walls of the castle loomed nearby, and Durell turned back toward the piazza where loudspeakers suspended from utility poles blared patriotic music. Evidently it was one of the countless Ethiopian holidays. He came out of the side street at a point from which he could see the railed balconies of the king's stone bathhouse. It was said Fasilidas drowned fair maidens there after a night's use of their bodies. Green and red lovebirds and long-tailed whydahs called among its ancient fig trees and cedars; lions roared in their cages close by.

Durell entered a stone doorway and pressed a call button in a nondescript *pensione*. He had never seen the fat, aged Greek who answered, but he knew that he had two sons and nine grandchildren in Chicago, and that he had visited them only the year before. That was when K Section, always on the alert for foreign residents amenable to American interests, had approached him. Bewildered, wary, a little frightened but also honored, the old man had assented to the use of his establishment as a haven for K Section agents should they ever have need of it. The possibility had seemed remote then. But now, by a sequence of events begun half a world away, Constantine Koidakis was at the vortex of a dark, deadly struggle he could not begin to comprehend.

Durell said: "Hello, John says Alexander is doing fine."

The old man blinked at him through thick, steel-rimmed

glasses and rubbed his hands on his big belly. "And the grandchildren?"

"Paul has graduated," Durell said, completing the recognition signals.

Koidakis glanced cautiously beyond Durell, then nodded toward the worn stairs. "Number five," he said.

"You're late. Run into trouble?"

"Some," Durell said. "How did it go with Tessema?"

"Perfectly," Hennessey said. The thin matress sagged under his thickly muscled bulk on an iron bedstead that trembled when he moved. He lay comfortably, coat off, tie loosened, propped up on pillows, sky-blue eyes smug and cunning. Durell took in the room at a glance. It was simply furnished: an ironware pitcher and bowl on a small washstand; a couple of straight-back, cane-bottom chairs; a huge pine wardrobe redolent of lavender sachet. Beside the bed a window looked out on the paizza where a green police VW passed among rickety Fiat taxis.

"You've sanitized the room?" Durell said.

"Yup. The only bugs have six legs."

A vague sense of unease troubled Durell's mind. He sat on the edge of the bed and said: "Did Mira contact you?"

"No. Is she in Gondar?" Hennessey sat up and the bedsprings squawked.

"She was at the hotel when I arrived last night. Then a guy served a hand grenade with my nightcap. No need to worry; she wasn't harmed. She just got the feeling that Asmara isn't the nice, safe town it used to be and decided to take a vacation. Anywhere would do."

"Geez, those bastards are really breathing down our necks, Cajun."

"Just feel above your collar once in a while to make sure you've still got your head on," Durell said. "Joseph Cesari, a Corsican mercenary, is their chief honcho. He offered me the toddy I missed at the hotel and wound up eating his glass."

"Did you wipe him?"

"I don't think so."

"He's a tough cookie," Hennessey said. "He's been

117

rumored all over Africa for years, from Rhodesia to the Sudan, wherever there's trouble. But he wouldn't be running the project."

"No, he's a hired gun. I left in a hurry and Mira picked me up. She wanted to come here with me, so I let her."

"Why isn't she with you, then?"

Durell sighed. Then he told Hennessey about the monarchists, Colonel Tekle and the message Mira had left in his coat pocket. "I figured she came on ahead to alert you about the meeting with Ineyu in case I couldn't get loose," he said.

"Some night you had," Hennessey said. "Well, she hasn't shown up here. I hope she's all right." He swung his feet off the bed with a bullish grunt, took his suitcase from the wardrobe and opened it on the mattress. "Here's the stuff you asked me to get from D.C.," he said, handing Durell five pages of notes written in a tight, neat hand. In spite of his huge size, Hennessey's penmanship showed that he was as finely coordinated as a watch, right down to his fingertips.

"The computer people at State weren't very happy about tackling this at four in the afternoon. Scared their dinner would get cold, I guess," Hennessey said.

"Paper pushers," Durell grumbled, scanning the notes.

Hennessey struck a match to a filter-tip cigarette and blew smoke at the ceiling. "Don't you ever wish you had a nice, eight-to-five job with nights on the free cocktail circuit?" he asked.

Durell ignored the question and glanced at his watch. He continued to sift through the facts and figures on Sinigaglia.

Hennessey said: "Sometimes I get fed up and tired; I just feel like chucking it."

"If you're tired, you should get out of the business," Durell said, not looking up.

"Yeah? How? Where do you go and what do you live on? What do the neighbors think when you always answer the door with a gun in your hand? Don't you ever think about the future, Cajun?"

Durell stared at him, his blue eyes darkening. "When

was the last time you stopped by D.C. for the routine psychological evaluation?"

Hennessey said: "I was scheduled two years ago, but I couldn't break away." He laughed. "Hey, don't go talking shrinks to me. Can't a man let his hair down with you once in a while?"

"Not when it comes to the business."

"You're a real company man, aren't you. Real, one hundred percent. Okay, so am I. But listen to me, Cajun: they can do without me; they can do without you. They can do without anybody you want to name."

Durell felt a surge of annoyance, but remained silent. He flipped back and forth through Hennessey's notes again and said, "I don't see the information developed from the SR-71 overflight here."

"Oh," Hennessey said offhandedly. "The flight was vetoed by State."

Durell grimaced. "Why?"

"State's afraid the spy plane might offend the Ethiopians unless they okay it. They're studying whether to ask. Knowing old Foggy Bottom, they'll make up their minds in six or eight weeks."

Durell spat an expletive. "I was counting on map coordinates from the flight to pinpoint the location of the blast. The satellite photo was too general for a fix."

"What about Tessema's recollections?"

"It's the best we have so far, but in those mountains a miss of a few miles could mean all the difference. We might be hunting for the Sinigaglia claim for weeks. Maybe Ineyu can add something. We can't wait for State to act."

Durell suddenly slapped the sheaf of notes with the back of his hand. "At least here's something. A Sinigaglia subsidiary was contracted five years ago by the French government. It supplied instrument technology for construction of a light water reactor, fuel processing plant and plutonium storage facility. It doesn't say where."

"I thought you'd be interested in that," Hennessey said. "If Sinigaglia has dealt with atomic power plants, maybe we're on the right track."

Durell glanced at his wristwatch again. It was nearly

119

three-thirty. "Let's get down to the lake," he said. "Ineyu may be our ace in the hole."

He just hoped Geza Della Gatta didn't hold a fistful of wild cards.

19

"We're being followed, Sam."

"I know."

Durell scanned the dun-colored grassland sloping south toward mile-high Lake Tana, still lost in the distance ahead. There were only knots of grazing lyre-horned cattle and occasional settlements of artisan Falashas, the landless Black Jews who traced their Hebrew heritage back to Solomon and Sheba.

No place to lose a determined shadow.

Durell had spotted the tail as it slipped into their wake on the piazza. Cars of American manufacture were scarce here, and this was a black Chevrolet stripped of chrome. It had the clean, anonymous look of a government vehicle just requisitioned from a motor pool.

Durell said: "It could be Colonel Tekle's Special Branch men."

Hennessey said: "That's what I'm afraid of." His big, pink hand slid under the lapel of his coat and withdrew a .38 Cobra revolver and laid it on the carpeted transmission-housing.

"Put it away," Durell said.

"You must be joking. Secret police are all alike—if they get hold of you, they'll turn you every way but loose."

"That's a chance we'll have to take. There's to be no gunplay. If Tekle nabs us on a solid rap, we'll be eating from a tin plate until our shoes rot off. He's obsessed with the monarchist threat, and he has the idea I'm working with them."

Hennessey's eyes plucked at the rear-vision mirror as

he replaced the pistol in his shoulder holster. The shoulder of the road reeled past in a reddish-brown blur. Durell glanced back, hot needles of sunlight piercing his eyes. The Chevrolet bored through the heat haze about 500 yards behind. It was impossible to tell who was in the car.

"What do you think, Cajun?" The strain of driving the hurtling Volvo made his voice brittle.

Durell thought briefly. The Chevrolet had not gained on them, but it had not fallen back, its driver maintaining his distance. It seemed reasonable to assume that he was under orders merely to keep them under surveillance and would avoid a fight.

"Make an emergency stop and head back the way we came. We can outrun him if you get away fast enough," he said. He locked his door against the off-chance of being thrown from the car. A minute passed as puffs of cloud drifted through the cerulean sky and dragged gray shadows over the grassland and highway. High up a shining tawny eagle went black as it soared into a slanting pillar of shade. Then the only car visible ahead passed by with a shout of torn air.

Hennessey hit the brakes. The Volvo's tires screamed as it tried to come end-around. Hennessey mastered it to a straight, dead stop that lasted only the fraction it took to pound it into reverse and lock the wheel all the way around to the left. He flattened the accelerator and the car careened in a backward half-spin.

"Look out!" Durell yelled.

The Chevrolet was almost on top of them, tires wailing.

At the last instant the little Volvo shot forward, beyond the deadly arc of the sliding Chevrolet's rear end, and sped away toward Gondar. Durell watched out the rear window as the black car slithered across the road and into the brown pastureland.

"We passed a cutoff to the Bahir Dar highway at Azczo," he said. "Take it, and we'll strike the lake on the east shore instead of at Gorgora. Our friend back there will have to guess which road to look for us on."

"Right."

Getting to Degas Island was more trouble than Durell had bargained for. The map lent him by Constantine Koidakis showed the highway following the eastern shore of the Rhode Island-size lake, but tropical foliage shrouded the water and only small villages of hippo-eating Waitos could be seen. He soon realized there was no hope of hiring a boat suitable for the trip to Degas unless they went all the way to Bahir Dar, where the Blue Nile tumbled from Tana's southern rim, or back to Gorgora. In light of their troubles back there, he opted for Bahir Dar. Time was racing past; he looked at his watch and knew they would never reach Ineyu by five o'clock.

By the time they arrived at the Bahir Dar boat docks he was dangerously impatient, his nerves sanded to raw stubs by the flow of lost minutes.

Bahir Dar, the Addis Ababa gateway to the island-studded lake, was a dingy tourist town doing a big business in cheap trinkets and fine Falasha pottery and textiles. Sightseers avoided Eritrea, but they still came here from all over the world, wholesome-looking Scandinavians, clannish Japanese and blithe Americans. For centuries the land of Prester John was a Christian island in a sea of Islam, shrouded in mystery. The mystery still tantalized, Durell reflected as he skirted a crowd boarding a tour boat.

He spoke to its black-capped master and came back to Hennessey and said, "The boat doesn't ordinarily stop at Degas, but the captain says he will put us ashore for a consideration."

"How much?" Hennessey asked. "Not that it matters."

"He was satisfied with five bucks American. Let's get aboard," Durell said.

They stood at the rail as the double-deck boat pulled sluggishly away from the docks, its muddy propeller wash slapping against the pilings. Nearly all of the tourists had opted for the upper deck, leaving Durell and Hennessey below with only one other passenger. Durell looked for the black Chevrolet as the landing receded, but it was not visible anywhere. He felt grateful for that, but his sense of relief was tainted by the knowledge that they had left the Volvo back there unhidden and undisguised, and that they must return to it after meeting Ineyu or find other transportation to Gondar.

A portentous silence hung over the immense gray lake. Hardly a cat's paw troubled its mountain reflections. The shore was still close, and Durell saw monkeys swing from vines trailing among the jungle trees. The boat passed within a few yards of a herd of hippos that sank to feed on the bottom, then rose blowing air. Crocodiles basked on the bank, and pythons moved along trails beaten among the papyrus reeds. Hundreds of egrets worked the glassy shallows. No fishermen were in view, but here and there they passed an adventurous tourist making for an island in a rented *tankwas* boat of papyrus reeds.

Then they were further out, and a haze filtered the shoreline into the blue spectrum. The throbbing of the engines came through the teak deck, and only the boat and the purling of water under its bow seemed real.

Durell heard a murmur of excited voices as they approached the first island. Tourists might have come to gaze on the waters that mothered the fabled Blue Nile, but the islands were the main attraction. The lake harbored nearly forty island monasteries founded in the Middle Ages, Durell remembered. Monks on some of the jungled islands guarded icons nearly two thousand years old, ancient church crowns and Bibles handwritten in Ge'ez, a dead religious language only a few could read. They watched over the mummified remains of King Fasilidas and the tombs of other notables from the dim past.

Durell felt a shudder as the tour boat reversed engines and struggled up to the landing. "Our island is next. Have you noticed our friend?" he said.

"Yup," Hennessey said. He sighed and leaned with his forearms crossed on the mahogany deck rail. He did not look at the dark-skinned man dressed in a tan suit who sat in a canvas chair near the fantail. "He was the last one aboard. He doesn't seem interested in the island. He isn't going ashore."

"There's doubtlessly another just like him waiting at the docks in Gorgora, in case we turned up there," Durell said, his eyes on a flight of crested cranes.

"How do you read him?" Hennessey said.

"Special Branch. If Colonel Tekle relayed Ineyu's message to Mira, then he knows the time and place of the meeting—maybe he even knows what it's about. But he can't figure where I fit into the picture. He must be getting curiouser and curiouser."

Hennessey stole a glance at the man, who sat with his back to them, commanding a view of all who disembarked. Hennessey said nothing more. When the landing party had disappeared into the foliage, the man climbed the steel gangway to the bridge. Durell and Hennessey looked at each other.

"There'll be a radiotelephone up there—he didn't have time to contact his pals from Bahir Dar," Durrell said.

A couple of minutes passed.

When the man returned to his deck chair, he did not seem interested in Durell and Hennessey.

Soon the boat's passengers embarked and the big craft churned away from the island.

The haze thickened into light fog and the shore could not be seen. The fog pillowed the hot rays of the late afternoon sun and shriveled it into a distinct yellow ball. Durell and Henessey leaned on the deck rail and looked into the graying mist. Abruptly the air was melodic with the tolling of bronze bells all around them, a twice-daily ritual of the monks. Durell reflected that the monasteries would be only ruins now, had it not been for a great battle fought on the shores here over four hundred years ago. That was when Ethiopian and Portuguese forces surprised and defeated Ahmed Gran and his Turkish riflemen, saving the country from a violent conversion to Islam.

The distant sound of a motorboat brought Durell's thoughts back to the present. Hennessey was no longer at his side. He knew instantly where the big man had gone and whirled toward the stern—but he was too late.

He glimpsed the dark-skinned man tumbling through the air, arms outstretched, fingers splayed wide.

Then the flailing form disappeared below the level of the deck.

Hennessey brushed his palms together and flashed Durell a deadly grin.

Durell could not see the man in the boat's gray-shrouded wake.

"We seem to have very different ideas about how to operate," Durell snapped angrily.

"How's that? You didn't tell me not to get rid of him," Hennessey said mildly.

"I thought you knew better than to kill him. That was stupid." Durell wanted to hit him, but he held it back, tried to quiet the fury that could lead to disastrous miscalculations.

"Well, maybe we should have brought a velvet chair for the bastard, too." Now Hennessey was surrendering to anger.

"If that was Tekle's man, there'll be hell to pay. I'll have to decide whether to hand you over to the authorities," Durell said.

Hennessey moved a step closer to Durell, his mountainous form seeming to block out everything, menace sparkling in his eyes. "On a murder rap? You wouldn't do that, Cajun."

"If need be, to save the mission," Durell said.

Henessey studied him, defiant but cautious, taking his measure. The look was a warning, like the bared fangs of a dog. Durell shifted his weight imperceptibly to the balls of his feet. He kept his arms loose at his sides, the only signals of danger his bolted jaw and darkening blue-black eyes.

Hennessey spat over the railing and grinned. "You're the chief, Cajun."

"Remember it."

Durell could not quite cap the anger that sputtered within. If the Special Branch man had got off with them on Degas, they could have taken care of him easily, without harming him. Durell could have sent Hennessey to lead him on a wild-goose chase, or they could have bound and stashed him and released him when they left. Either way, they could have been gone before he brought others.

Degas Island loomed suddenly close beyond the port rail. The green wall of vegetation was all blacks and grays in the mist. A breeze had sprung up and it blew drizzle onto Durell's cheeks, chill and sad as a mourner's fingers.

The tourists began to descend to the bottom deck, hiding from the damp. They watched with curiosity as Durell and Hennessey strode quickly across the gangplank onto a low stone bank and disappeared behind curtains of fog and jungle.

Both big men had looked frightfully earnest.

Even angry.

20

Durell heard the throb of the tour boat's diesels as they powered the craft away, leaving him alone with Hennessey and whatever lay ahead. The boat would not return. They would get back to the mainland by the transportation Ineyu had brought, Durell decided.

To all outward appearances, the island was uninhabited.

Insects whirred angrily amid the splattering of dripping water in the overhanging foliage. Things slithered in the dank shadows as they followed a weedy tunnel through the jungle uphill, away from a rotted pier. Durell pressed ahead through clutching twigs and thorns. Hennessey cursed as branches slapped him with dew-laden leaves. The smell of toads and decay poisoned their breathing, the air turgid down among the vines and brush. Both men soon were soaked with water and sweat, their hands marked by scratches, their shoes slimed with mud.

Then they came to the edge of the woods, and Durell motioned for Hennessey to stop. Waist-high vegetation clogged an old clearing in front of them. A flight of Egyptian geese winged overhead, fog diminishing their bright colors. Durell held his gun with quiet competence and carefully regarded the ancient stone monastery there. A huge banyan tree shrouded a corner. Saplings and weeds grew from the detritus on its flat roof. Creepers spread black veins along its walls, probed its dark window sockets.

The monastery was high on a promontory overlooking the lake. Unfettered by the jungle up here, the wind flayed the crumbling structure with swirling mist. Tattered kaba leaves rattled against its stones.

If Ineyu were anywhere on the island, it would be here, Durell decided.

"Circle around back. Come in that way, and I'll link up with you inside," he whispered.

Hennessey brought the .38 Cobra out of his coat and said: "Ineyu should be alone, unless Mira's in there with him."

"Things are damned seldom the way they should be," Durell said.

Hennessey crept away, bending low beside the wall of jungle. The vegetation swallowed his oversized bulk soundlessly. Durell crouched, hearing only the wind, the click and hum of insects, the leafy patter of a light rain shower that had begun falling. He counted slowly to ten, then moved rapidly across the clearing. Crumbled mortar, a weathered, fallen door cluttered the gloomy entrance. A bright green lizard scurried from underfoot as he stepped over the threshold and into the musty shadows.

He went through an alcove and into a long hallway and thought he smelled cigarette smoke in the intolerably humid air. The silence seemed bound in steel.

He grasped his revolver loosely as he moved cautiously down the corridor, alert for the snap of a straw, the scrape of a shoe. The hall cut sharply to the left, then descended five stone steps to a wide landing. Beyond was the somber murk of a chapel. Durell stepped inside and a pearllike speck caught his gaze from the far end of the room.

Durell recognized the white of a man's eye reflecting the dismal light, the shape of a dark head.

The Ethiopian sat on the bare floor, his back against a wall frescoed with a primitive rendering of Adam and Eve in the Garden of Eden.

Durell aimed at the man. "Ineyu?"

"Yes?"

127

"Cajun here."

The man's eyes found him across the shadows and Durell saw a helpless, hunted look on his face. He realized all at once that something was terribly wrong.

"Run!" Ineyu shouted.

Durell half-turned, glimpsed the blur of an arm.

Then something crashed violently against the back of his skull. The next instant, he was on all fours, riding a roller coaster over a black chasm of unconsciousness. Pain spewed in his head like hot blood from a sundered artery. He blinked and fought to pull the shattered core of his awareness toegther again

Hands yanked him to his feet. The cold ring of a gun muzzle was pressed just above his navel. Cesari's face, inches away, leered hatefully at him.

Tape and gauze plastered the cuts Durell had inflicted, disfiguring jaw and cheeks. Too late, he recognized the odor of the Corsican's Alpha cigarettes. Half a dozen men armed with handguns backed up the sleek, pugnacious mercenary. Durell did not know where they had come from, unless the monks' cells behind or the chapel windows.

"How I would like to kill you," Cesari hissed, his eyes bloody fires.

"You're lucky to get a second chance—what's stopping you?" Durell heard his own words woven with strident ringing in his punished brain. Adam and Eve seemed to dance obscenely in their faded paradise on the wall.

"There has been a change of plan. You will come with us."

He had no choice but to obey.

"They were waiting for me when I got here," Ineyu said.

"Silence!" Cesari barked.

They descended a long, irregular stairway carved from the living rock beneath the floor of the monastery. Ineyu's coffee brown eyes shown balefully beneath heavy brows and his obstinate lips were drawn tight. Strands of gray marbled his woolly black hair; his five-day-old beard was dusted with silver. He was no youngster, Durell reflected.

His ordeal in the mountains seemed to have taken more out of his stalwart frame than he could spare. Grime darkened his checkered flannel shirt; his whipcord slacks were torn at the knee.

Durell wondered where Hennessey was. The monks of old had made an amateurish effort to hide the staircase entrance. Hennessey would find it easily enough, but common sense argued against a rescue attempt by only one man. The odds against its success were overwhelming. If Hennessey followed procedure, he would not risk himself and the mission. Escape would be up to Durell.

The stairs ended in a damp-floor cavern. Light from kerosene lanterns flickered on rippled stone walls and brightened ribbons of water-deposited minerals to gold. Bat guano cut at the nostrils with the stench of ammonia. Webs of shadow hung in the distant reaches where Durell suspected side caverns, if only he could get to them.

They passed a glistening pillar of flowstone and turned into a spacious room carved by the force of ancient subterranean torrents. The mouth of an immense pit gaped in the floor. A battery-powered wireless was nearby.

"Bring him to me." The command was in Italian, the voice cold with the knowledge of absolute authority. Durell's eyes sought the speaker beyond a frozen curtain of dripstone.

On one of six marble tombs sunk into the moist earth towered the thin form of Geza Della Gatta, sharp shoulders hunched like a vulture's, the stringy rope of his neck bent under a sharp, brutal chin. Durell sensed an aura of enormous power and merciless cruelty about the man and thought of the thousands who had died at his hands, the millions perhaps to come. The Italian's cold, bullet eyes bespoke a madness that could not be satisfied with less than the power to control life and death for everyone on the planet.

He was carelessly dressed in knee-length, lace-up boots, jodhpurs, and ill-fitting dark coat, as if impatient of such mundane considerations in his dark quest. The only outward show of vanity was a .357 Colt revolver hanging from his thin waist in an embossed leather holster. It was silvered and had pearl grips, and Della Gatta rested the

129

heel of his bony hand on its butt in paranoiac readiness to kill at the slightest provocation.

"Now you are mine," he said.

"Only if you can hold me," Durell said flatly.

"You are impudent."

"And you are mad."

Della Gatta sneered in the fiery lantern light. "Who is to say? Common definitions have no meaning, common restraints no longer apply, once affairs transcend certain boundaries."

"Power has its own morality? You're still spouting the same Fascist crap that brought on the Second World War, Della Gatta."

"The Fascists were on the right path. I shall do better," Della Gatta said.

"By blowing up the world?"

"You know of our project, of course—it seems no place is safe from the prying eyes of the great powers." The man shook his bony face slowly, his arrogant Roman nose brassy in the lamplight. "I do not intend to blow up the world, Mr. Durell. It shall be spared, so long as it pays the price. Of course, there will be initial casualties, as a show of strength . . . "

"Where did you get the fissionable material?" Durell asked. The longer he could keep Della Gatta talking, the better chance Hennessey had of getting off the island.

Della Gatta might have smiled. "That information can be of no value to you—now," he said thinly.

"If you get rid of me others will come," Durell said.

"You will call off your K Section dogs and I will not get rid of you," Della Gatta said simply.

"There's no way you'll get me to do that."

"We shall see. In a few days we will leave Ethiopia. The first contingent of weapons will be in channels of distribution. Once dispersed they will be sufficient deterrent to further pursuit. Organizations all over the world will pay a princely sum for just one of them. I have no desire to involve myself in the political squabbles to which they will be applied, but I shall retain control of the means of production and, by that, the ultimate power."

Durell felt a tremor of revulsion at the hideous prospect

of terrorists with atomic bombs. The menace was incalculable. Della Gatta was even more inhuman than he had thought.

"It's a golden opportunity for you," Della Gatta said in his slow, sinister voice. "With your experience and natural abilities, I may allow you to join me. You see, the weapons must be entrusted to men who are essentially untrustworthy, men whose only allegiance to me is as a source of the product."

"So you need an enforcer—an assassin. You're already living with the fear of those who rule by terror. Give it up. With your wealth you've got everything a reasonable man could ask."

"There is nothing left but to move beyond wealth."

"I won't help you."

"That is up to you. Bind his hands."

Durell did not resist. He held his wrists together in front of his belt, and Della Gatta's men, rushing to obey, tied them there, where he would at least have some use of them. The thin cord was jerked tightly into the flesh of his forearms.

"Make your choice," Della Gatta said. "Tell your embassy there is no further cause for alarm, that a full report will follow to K Section on your return to the United States. Once you betray them, you will have no alternative but to come over to me." He paused, waiting, then said: "What will it be?"

"Cram it."

Della Gatta made a nodding motion with his narrow face. Hands came from everywhere. Durell was half-dragged across the cavern and he remembered the pit and thought dimly of the suffocating waters far below, the breathtaking plummet to oblivion. Every breath, every note of living tissue in his body suddenly was a thing to cherish. But they carried him beyond the pit to one of the tombs, where eight men muscled the cover aside. He looked down and saw that the dark slot was filled almost to the top with stagnant, foul-smelling water, the seepage of ages over decaying remains.

He controlled his horror as his feet were lifted abruptly from the ground and he was laid in the odious cavity, his back against the bones of some long-dead nobleman. He could keep his face out of the water only by supporting himself on his elbows.

Then the men shoved the massive lid back into place.

He stilled an impulse to lash out; stemmed the burst of panic, told himself to calm down, save his energy.

Durell knew that he could never budge that slab by himself.

He took refuge in the thought that Della Gatta had not killed him outright and decided the ruthless Italian still hoped to get what he wanted from him.

Or he might have departed, written Durell off, left him to die and molder in the lost burial chamber where not even his remains would ever be found.

21

Yellow images floated into Durell's vis-ion, then dissolved in the chill murk. He could hear his shallow breathing against the marble slab two inches from his mouth. The muscles of his abdomen, back and arms quivered with the effort of holding his face out of the fetid water. The points of his elbows ached where his weight rested on them.

He had lost all sense of time.

But he knew he could not sustain himself much longer.

Only an inbred will to survive and the possibility of release kept him alive minute by interminable minute.

Maybe Della Gatta was putting him through this torment in hopes of breaking him, but clearly it mattered little to him if Durell died in the process. Most men would be dead already, and still the tomb's cover remained in place. The slab lay ponderously over him, tongue in groove with the tomb's sides and nearly airtight. The atmosphere had turned stale in seconds. Now it was rancid, polluted dangerously by the carbon dioxide Durell had exhaled. He had lost great amounts of body heat to the cold water and hypothermia threatened as the temperature in the core of his vital organs subsided toward fatal levels.

Then he passed out.

It lasted only a fraction of a second, but it was a warning that the end was imminent. He awoke when his nostrils filled with the bitter water, lurched up, banged his head against the stone lid, coughed and retched. The putrid water sloshed in deadly little waves over his mouth and cheeks and eyes. He held himself rigid. His body screamed for respite. Gradually, the dark water calmed.

He could hardly draw a satisfactory breath now. The oxygen trapped in the airspace was nearly depleted. He gasped as shudders of fatigue and exposure racked his frame. He could buy some time by relaxing totally, keeping his body's demand for oxygen at the lowest possible point. But if he released the tension in his muscles, his head would sink backwards and he could drown.

He remembered the dead nobleman's bones.

He rolled facedown in the grisly water and clawed at the broken skeleton with his bound hands, pushing the bones toward the head of the tomb. The rib cage had collapsed but the skull was large and solid. With the pelvis and heavy leg bones the remains made enough of a pillow to cradle his face barely above the water in the fetid air space.

He relaxed his cramped muscles, his hopes somewhat revived. He kept his arms and legs close and tried to preserve as much body heat as possible.

Even if Della Gatta remained out there, even if he opened the tomb and let him rise from the dead, he could never do the man's bidding, Durell reflected. He would die anyway.

There was only one satisfaction.

Among the bones Durell had encountered a ceremonial dagger, buried with its owner. The blade had not rusted, and he judged it was made of silver. He slipped the weapon inside his shirt and lay with bound hands clasped over it.

If they lifted the tomb's cover, Geza Della Gatta would be his mark.

The nectar-sweet scent of fresh air caressed Durell's nostrils and he struggled up from some dim, terminal sleep. He had lost consciousness again; he did not know for how long. The time lapse could have stretched into eternity for all he would have known. Now he heard the ragged scrape of the lid and a thin, orange strip of light appeared above his eyes.

They had come to take him out.

There came heavy grunts as the opening widened.

Then they hauled him out of the obscene water and back to Della Gatta near the lip of the pit. The air blew the fuzz from his brain; strength rebounded into his tough fibres. He glimpsed Ineyu standing with bound hands beside the hole in the cavern floor, his dark eyes watchful.

On a stone ledge beyond Ineyu was a compact radio-telephone in a white cabinet of high-impact plastic, its antenna lead running back toward the stairs to the monastery. The device had been brought down as Durell struggled for his life in the tomb.

The coppery light glinted on Della Gatta's teeth and his voice was malevolent as he said: "Are you prepared to cooperate? You shall have no more reprieves."

"No." Durell estimated the distance between them at six feet and knew he would never get across that space alive. If only his hands were not bound, he could throw the knife. . . .

"You *will* do it," Della Gatta said evenly.

Durell moved a step closer, his hands over the hidden dagger. "Don't bet on it," he said. He started to move again and felt the hard touch of a pistol at his temple.

"Keep your distance or I'll blow your brains out," Cesari said harshly.

"Take him to the transmitter," Della Gatta commanded. "We will place the call via the radiotelephone switchboard in Addis Ababa, Mr. Durell. Then you will say what you have been told—or die on the spot. *Signor*

134

Cesari anticipates the latter eventuality with immense pleasure, I assure you."

Durell's heart sank as he despaired of killing Della Gatta. It was senseless to lunge for him only to be shot down before he could strike home.

Cesari stepped to one side and fanned the air with his pistol, motioning Durell toward the transceiver.

Durell turned reluctantly, his eyes swiveling across the chamber to Ineyu. He felt the Corsican's gun against his spine, broke the contact with a step and went slowly toward the red "on" light of the transmitter, beyond the sinkhole's black maw.

His instinct winnowed and weighed perceptions—danger, distance, minute fragments of seconds—feeding a torrent of subconscious impulses into his superbly polished sense of timing.

"Looks like you're on top, Cesari," he said.

"*Oui, monsieur*. It was destined to be." Cesari's voice was gloating.

They were approaching Ineyu. "Destiny can play tricks," Durell said.

"I will not make another mistake with you."

How far behind him was the Corsican: a step? Two? At what angle was the gun pointed? The light was poor—for how many milliseconds would surprise count?

The controls in Durell's brain screamed with tension; then he launched himself sideways, rammed Ineyu with his shoulder and they plummeted head over heels into the vast, dusky pit.

Above him came the crack of a pistol, the shocked roar of Della Gatta's voice: "Fool!"

The tumbling, spinning fall seemed interminable. Durell held his breath and clenched his teeth and felt his stomach turn into a giddy void as the wind rushed past his face. He curled into a ball, chin tucked against his chest, hoping only that he would not smash against the wall and be crushed. Then he slammed into the pool below with a jolting splash. Immediately he heard a second impact as Ineyu struck the surface. Durell groped for the knife, stuck it in his belt and sawed his bonds loose as he sank in a fizz of swirling bubbles. He found Ineyu orbiting downward and cut his hands free, then gave him a yank to show that he should follow him in the drift of current down there.

Durell heard bullets spank the surface. He did not rise for air, but followed an enormous submarine duct. He hoped it connected with the lake, but it might also descend into an underground river where their bodies would be swept helplessly away.

A bare suggestion of watery light glimmered ahead. There was the slimy touch of bottom plants, the stalks of reeds. Roiling sediment darkened the water and Durell realized why when he bumped the massive, yielding body of a feeding hippo. He recoiled, arched to the surface, shook the water from his face and inhaled deeply of the warm, misty air. Ineyu's head bobbed up next to him. The Ethiopian coughed and gasped for breath.

It was nearing dusk. High above, the monastery loomed darkly through a blowing drizzle. The wind beat on the water and whitecaps shone dully through the gloom. Durell saw they were only twenty or thirty yards from the densely wooded shore—and that some of the same men they had just fled were pushing a papyrus reed boat from the shelter of trees onto the lake. They had known of the underwater passage.

A pistol cracked and spume flew into the air a yard to Durell's left.

He waited a few more seconds, catching his breath.

Three more bullets slapped the surface; a gust of wind blew sounds of the shots away in the smoky gray air. Four men had the boat in the water and were boarding it. Ineyu looked exhausted, but there was no help for it.

"Head around the point of the island," Durell called. "Maybe we can lose them for a moment and get back to shore. It'll be dark soon." He set off with a powerful crawling stroke as the men paddled furiously to close the distance. Ineyu fell behind at once.

Suddenly there was the explosion of a hand grenade, the kick of an underwater shock wave, the hiss of droplets streaming back into the frothing lake. Durell glanced back, beyond where Ineyu stroked in leaden rhythm.

The boat advanced toward him as lightly as a water

spider, its bow cutting the chop. One of the men cocked his arm to hurl another grenade. Then the boat seemed to strike something, veered abruptly, lifted its bows to the stormy sky and capsized.

Only then did Durell see the hippos: the blast of the grenade had stampeded them.

With incredible agility and power, the rubbery mountains of flesh surged to the surface, snapping and kicking, spewing spray and churning the lake to foam. The men flailed helplessly amid the furious animals; giant jaws snapped and a cry was cut to a smothered gasp. With single-minded violence the hippos focused their attack on the boat, pig's eyes gleaming as they bit and thrashed the frail craft to splinters. The four men suffered almost incidentally, rammed by lunging jaws or crushed between leviathan bodies.

Durell waited off to one side until Ineyu reached him. The Ethiopian's breathing was harsh with exhaustion. Durell was sustained by what seemed to be his last reserves of energy.

"Head for shore," he panted.

Suddenly, he heard the whine of jet turbines, helicopter blades pounding the air. He looked into the blowing mist and spotted the dark form of a huge, black-painted Sikorsky S-61L low to the water, without running lights, banking toward them.

He felt stuck in the water, his progress toward the shore agonizingly slow before the onrushing helicopter.

His toes touched mud; he slipped and his head went under. He gained another yard, found the bottom again and the silt clutched him to the ankle with a slimy suck. Ineyu struggled beside him, his breath coming in rapid puffs.

It was no use. The helicopter was almost on top of them, so low that Durell could see the evil visage of Della Gatta in the green radiance of cockpit lights. They were utterly vulnerable. He could annihilate them before they reached the shelter of the bank.

In rage and despair Durell thought of hurling the silver burial knife at the windshield.

But then, incredibly, the giant Sikorsky spun about and soared away into the mist.

Dazed, Durell stood on the muddy bottom, chest heaving with ragged gasps of air, eyes fixed on the point where the craft had vanished in the drizzle. He felt Ineyu nudge his elbow and followed the Ethiopian's narrowed gaze. The sweep of his vision told him the hippos had quieted. He saw no survivors from the reed boat. Some fifty yards away a white-painted whaleboat cut the lake toward them. Beyond it loomed the dim shape of a cutter, its profile suggesting an American-made minesweeper of World War II vintage.

They stood silently, rivulets of water streaming out of their hair and down their faces, as the whaleboat eased up beside them.

A young officer in army uniform stood up in its bow. Durell's eyes hardened as he saw the brass insignia on the officer's collar.

It was that of the dreaded Special Branch—bossed by the same Colonel Mamo Tekle who had threatened to shoot him just that morning.

22

Still clad in their soggy clothes, Durell and Ineyu sipped black coffee from heavy mugs and huddled under woolen blankets in the small officers' mess of the cutter. An armed sailor stood at the entrance to the compartment.

"Tekle's got it in for me. This could get nasty," Durell said in a low voice.

"I don't think so; I know Colonel Tekle," Ineyu replied calmly.

"Can you handle him?"

Ineyu stared at Durell from under heavy brows. "Maybe," he said.

Durell scruitinized the stoutly built man and decided he showed every measure of competence; he looked tough to the bone.

Durell sipped his coffee thankfully. He wondered where the cutter was headed and judged no place good with Tekle in charge. The colonel had him labeled as a monarchist conspirator because of his hapless contracts with Ambaw; Ineyu would be lucky not to be tarred with the same brush, he thought.

He did not speak to Ineyu again. He had risked being overheard as much as he dared. Anything else they had to say was not for Tekle's ears.

Night blacked the sky and the enfolding mist blotted out stars and shore lights as the cutter crept with caution through the mile-high chill of fog and rain. Only the sense of smell betrayed a world beyond the vessel. Durell scented the lake's fishy odor mixed with that of honey and woodshavings from islands lying hidden and treacherous in the fog.

"Well, Captain Worota, did you miss your connection with Miss Seragate?"

Durell looked up and saw the fox-faced Tekle stride briskly through the compartment's hatch. His fatigues looked as crisply starched as they had that morning. He laid his rhinoceros-hide riding crop on the steel dining table, sat down and folded his arms.

"I gave her your message this morning," he continued, "and she must have sent this monarchist gunrunner to make trouble. One can never trust a beautiful woman, especially with a man who has been so gallant as to lend her his coat. Did you think I wouldn't notice that you wore the same coat, Mr. Durell? Naturally, we had you followed when you commandeered the Volkswagen." He smiled. It was not pleasant.

Then he said: "How unfortunate that the helicopter could not pick you up—and how ironic that I plucked you from the water, when you threw one of my men into it from the tour boat."

Without replying to Tekle, Durell regarded Ineyu—a captain in the Special Branch. Only the deepest loyalties carried one through the dangerous, sometimes loath-

139

some tasks of his profession, he thought. It was not a quality that a man could easily give two masters. There was the hazard of conflict, a desperate moment of choosing, and one side or the other would suffer. He wondered if Ineyu had reached that crossroads.

"You'd better spell it out for me, *Captain*. Point by point," he said bitterly.

"Spell it out for both of us," Tekle said. He slapped his quirt against the table. "Why have you been out of contact for five days? And why does this Durell speak to you as if he is your superior?"

Ineyu turned his face to Durell. Only the muted flicker of inner strife shone in his eyes. "Do I have permission? The situation is desperate. I think it is what we must do."

Durell's permanent Q clearance allowed him to operate as he deemed necessary. He hadn't expected this, but he could use the powerful colonel's help in getting to Della Gatta. As good a chance of obtaining it might not come again. He nodded almost imperceptibly to Ineyu.

Ineyu said: "Colonel Tekle, let me introduce Samuel Durell, chief field agent for K Section."

Tekle sat bolt upright. Anger darkened his face.

"Let me explain, sir," Ineyu said. "There are some things you do not know, and some Mr. Durell does not know. It begins with the monarchists. My mission against them was approved at the highest levels by both of our governments. In fact, Mr. Durell's superior, General Dickinson McFee, chose me for the task. I was trained for intelligence work by the U.S. during the Korean War. I received my commission in army intelligence while serving with the Kagnew Battalion of the Imperial Bodyguard, supplied by our country to the United Nations Command. The present regime reactivated my commission when I was selected to penetrate the monarchist movement.

"I was to subvert them using American dollars supplied by K Section. The funds could be traced only to Washington, which enhanced my credibility as a U.S. agent. I told them the Americans wanted to restore the monarchy, with which it had been on good terms. And I gave them money to prove my sincerity. Mira assisted me, and we gained their confidence.

"We compiled quite a list of counterrevolutionaries. And we slowly uncovered their power structure. We recently pinpointed *Dejasmatch* Nadu Ambaw as their leader.

"As you may know, sir, he has considerable holdings in the Semien Mountains. For generations his family has wielded great power there. It is a huge, poorly known territory, but I had learned the rough location of the seat of *Dejasmatch* Ambaw's estates. I concluded that it would be the focus of a gathering of monarchist forces. I chartered a plane and flew over the area to pinpoint it. My landmark was to be the Sinigaglia mining concession, which I had learned was nearby and leased from *Dejasmatch* Ambaw."

Ineyu continued, telling Tekle of the atomic blast and the forced landing. He said Ambaw's tribesmen took him into custody at gunpoint as he went for help; that he escaped the next night and began his long trek out of the mountains. Evidently word of his presence reached those who had detonated the nuclear device, he said, because he had to hide by day from helicopters that searched for him.

Tekle appeared dumbfounded; his pointed jaw hung open as if unhinged. "So, it was these atomic outlaws who attacked you at Degas Island?"

"Yes, sir," Ineyu said. "They are led by a wealthy Italian, Geza Della Gatta."

Durell said: "Ferry me and Ineyu into the mountains by helicopter. We can reconnoiter his hideout as well as Ambaw's. If you strike there blindly, you may get the monarchists, but there is every chance that Della Gatta will escape in the confusion."

"Very well," Tekle said. "You will carry a wireless. When the stage is set, signal us. A platoon of airborne troops will be standing by their helicopters. I can provide your supplies. When do you wish to leave?"

"We must arrive there under cover of darkness. How about 0300 hours tomorrow?" Durell said.

"Consider it done."

After a dinner of beef steak and beer aboard the cutter, a staff car hurried Durell and Ineyu from the Gorgora lakefront to the safe house in Gondar. The mucky weather seemed to have germinated in the vast lake, then surged over the entire countryside. The fog, laden with smells of damp grain and the manure of lyre-horned cattle, groped its way into the city, where the piazza still echoed with strident music and speeches from the loudspeakers.

Despite the hot meal, relaxation did not come easily to Durell. The tension of his past and future encounters with Geza Della Gatta and his murderous Corsican henchman bound his muscles up like catgut.

It was almost 10 P.M. when their driver dropped them off at the Greek's *pensione*. The dour mass of King Fasilidas's castle shone through the drizzle, light traffic easing in a ribbon of headlamp beams past its parade ground. The night was fringed with the violent chortle of hyenas as they came down from the hills and fed on garbage in the alleys.

"Mr. Koidakis?" Durell knocked on the concierge's door. A moment passed, then the door opened cautiously. The man peered at Durell through the thick plugs of his steel-rimmed glasses.

"Ah, Cajun." the old grandfather seemed to relish using Durell's code name. "I will get your key."

"Any messages? I lost Hennessey somewhere," Durell said.

"Haven't heard from him, sir."

"There is a woman—Mira Seragate. Has she contacted you?"

"No, sir. No trouble, I hope."

"I don't know. Tell me immediately if you hear from either of them."

The room appeared untouched. Covers on the rickety iron bedstead were wrinkled with the imprint of Hennesseys big frame; the cane-bottom chairs fitted exactly into Durell's mental picture of how the room had been left. Nothing was disturbed in the old-fashioned pine wardrobe. The lavender sachet made Durell feel almost as much at home as anywhere in his shadowy, lonely wanderings.

Ineyu lay on the bed with a brief groan.

"Are you all right?" Durell asked. "You look feverish."

"Don't worry about me," Ineyu said.

Durell removed only his coat and shoes. He lay down in the darkness as church bells tolled ten o'clock. The snarl of a caged lion came through the window; the rip of a motorbike engine; a donkey's bray. Music, distant and confused, sounded from row upon row of bars on the road opposite the Arab market.

"Cajun?"

"Yes."

"I was inducted into the Special Branch after McFee approved my mission against the monarchists. I hadn't expected it; it's detestable to me."

"When the politicians get together, no one knows what to expect," Durell said bleakly. He knew that McFee, no less than Ineyu, must be only a tool of higher-ups in this monarchist thing. Someone very near the top must have approved it in hopes of making friends with the new regime.

Ineyu said: "I hate the military and the monarchists. One day we will have democracy like you. We may have to fight for that. If we do, I shall call in your debts to me."

"I'll do whatever I can—you'd better get some rest now."

Durell lay awake long after Ineyu's breathing lengthened into the deep, regular inhalations of sleep. The loudspeakers had gone silent and the city quieted. He watched car lights mingle across the ceiling, the tires hissing on the wet thoroughfare below. Timbers creaked as the night sucked the heat of the tropical sun out of the roof.

A vague unease troubled his mind, a sense of something left undone—or perhaps yet to come.

He thought of Hennessey's valise and notes. The bag was in Koidakis's safekeeping; the papers had been destroyed before they left for the lake. Everything had been taken care of. It left only the coming hours to worry about. But he had no way of seeing into the future.

He slipped from the bed and checked the locks on door and windows with care. They were secure.

He returned to the bed and closed his eyes.

Durell awoke with the first knock on the door.

He did not know how long he had slept, but his mind was alert, his body refreshed. It seemed too early for the Special Branch driver to call.

"Who is it?" he asked, his hand on the doorknob.

"Me, sir. Constantine Koidakis."

Durell pulled the door open. The old man's eyes were puffy with sleep. A hand clutched his flannel robe together over his rotund belly.

"My apologies, sir, but . . ." He thrust a sealed envelope into Durell's hand. It was addressed to Hennessey.

"What's this?"

"A courier from your embassy in Addis Ababa brought it. Since Mr. Hennessey is not here, I thought . . ."

"Right." Durell tore the envelope open and read the message on a single sheet of paper inside. He cursed in a low voice. "This authorizes the French *Service de Documentation Exterieure et de Contre-Espionnage* to team on our assignment."

"Ah." Koidakis nodded.

Durell scanned the paper again. "It reads like the agent is supposed to contact us—just as everything is set, I guess we're expected to put it on hold and sit."

"But . . ." Koidakis began.

"Here, burn this." Durell crumpled the message into a ball and pressed it into the Greek's hand. "What time is it?"

Koidakis glanced at his old-fashioned Gruen wristwatch. "Two-seventeen, sir, but . . ."

"Our colleague has forty-three minutes to get here. We won't postpone."

"Sir! I've been trying to tell you. Someone is waiting downstairs."

144

"Let's go," Durell growled. His patience was at an end.

He wondered with some perplexity where the French fit into it. If they were as deeply involved in the pursuit of Della Gatta as he, where had they been all this time? But if their investigation had just started, what could they possibly add?

Then, an instant before Koidakis opened the door to his downstairs quarters, the realization dawned.

He looked beyond the wide figure of the Greek. "You!"

"You!" she echoed.

It was Deste Giroud.

A tumult of conflicting emotions shook Durell's mind as he regarded the stunned, childlike face of the woman who stood there in tan gabardine slacks and forest green safari jacket. She had pulled her long, golden tresses back into a roll of businesslike severity. The gravity of her resolve was reinforced by the bulge of a shoulder holster under her arm.

She took an uncertain step toward him, but checked herself when he made no response.

Old Koidakis looked from one to the other, aware that the mingling of their gaze was laden with unspoken meaning. He cleared his throat and said, "I'll make some coffee." He stopped at the threshold and glanced back. Neither Durell nor Deste had moved.

When they were alone, Deste said: "I expected a Mr. Thomas Hennessey."

"It would have been better."

"Sam? Why?" Wonder polished the old silver of her eyes.

"I can't work with you; I don't trust you."

"Didn't I help you escape from Ambaw's encampment last night? Do you really prefer always to be alone?"

"I prefer to endanger no one but myself—and not to chance betrayal. Last night was one thing, Asmara another. You just as good as put the gun to my head at Ambaw's villa. How do I know what you will do next?"

Deste's lips tightened. "In reply to that, I can only say you have your orders." She made a small sound of dis-

145

tress, and said, "Dear Sam, listen to me. I have no interest in the monarchists and never did. I had to betray you to Ambaw, don't you see? It was a golden opportunity to prove myself to him. I doubt that I would ever have got into the mountains with him any other way, and I had to find the Sinigaglia claim. Besides, I had every intention of helping you escape before dark."

"And what if he had killed me on the spot?"

"It was a chance I had to take, Sam."

Durell nodded thoughtfully. He did not like it, but he understood. It was what he might have done himself, if a mission made it necessary. No matter how close a relationship seemed, the gulf of duty always lay between. At least Deste was aware of that uncomplicated fact, willing to live for the moment and put the treacherous future out of her mind. He should be grateful for that, he decided.

He lifted her chin on his knuckles and regarded her mirrored eyes. "There will be dying," he said.

She put her arms around him, her body reviving memories. "I'm familiar with death. Just don't let it be you."

Durell pushed her away gently as Koidakis brought in coffee. He poured, then left them with the china pot.

"How did the SDECE get involved in this?" Durell asked.

"Our government made the mistake of selling a nuclear power plant and fuel reprocessing facilities to the African state of Pakuru. We didn't publicize the deal, naturally, because we broke the rules—all of the atomic powers at that time required that spent fuel rods be turned back to them for processing so that the plutonium derived from them could not be used for weapons by the countries buying their plants. But in Pakuru we constructed the complete cycle, the generating plant, the light water fuel processing plant and even a storage facility for plutonium as a by-product by the plant. The plutonium was to be sold to France and the reprocessed uranium put back into the plant's fuel chain. But our controls were lax, and I'm afraid Della Gatta bribed officials to divert some of the plutonium to him. One of his subsidiaries held a contract for instrumentation on the project, so he had ample cover to visit the country and deal behind the scenes."

Durell listened glumly. He knew Pakaru only too well. Some years before he had saved the throne of its ruthless head of state, Prince Atimboku Mari Mak Mujilikaka. Later a multinational race for the Zero Formula had pitted him against the Yale-educated prince, by then dissolute and wealthy, and Durell had shot him and left him to die in the jungles of the Amazon. Prince Tim's beautiful sister, golden-eyed Salduva Hukkim, had taken the reins of government. For a moment Durell's thoughts went back to Sally, the "Queen Elephant," and their last night together under the equatorial stars of Belém.

"It was stupid to supply reprocessing facilities to Prince Tim," he said flatly.

"It has tremendous riches in its diamond and copper mines," Deste said. "The sale of nuclear generating plants has become big business among governments. Competition is fierce. In Pakuru we'd hoped to establish a model of what we could do for other developing countries."

"Instead you've shown what can happen through the unrestrained and unregulated spread of nuclear technology."

Durell judged that smuggling sufficient amounts of plutonium would not be difficult, given proper safeguards against radiation. It took less than twelve pounds of the diabolically destructive element to fashion a crude atomic bomb. He conjectured that Della Gatta's money had bought easy complicity of guards and bureaucrats in diverting weapons-grade material from the plant's fuel chain—and that the corrupt appointees of the late ruler still had an arrangement with the Italian. After all, Prince Tim had built an immense personal fortune on Pakuru's new-found mineral wealth, while his countrymen had remained impoverished.

"We've begun to set things straight," Deste said. "Without our assistance the plant cannot operate, and we have withdrawn our technicians. We have no means to punish Pakuran officials, of course."

"I suspect the Elephant Queen will settle matters there," Durell said.

"We followed the trail of the plutonium to Ethiopia. You know the rest of the story," Deste said.

Durell was grim. "Let's just hope it doesn't end in a holocaust," he said.

Deste spoke with determination. "We shall prevent that. We must."

23

The sound of dripping water came through the flimsy walls of the clapboard briefing hut. Steel folding chairs sat about in no particular arrangement. Muddy footprints smudged the wooden floor. A neatly ruled blackboard listed the day's flights. Durell's was not on it.

He, Ineyu, Deste, Tekle and a chain-smoking pilot stood around a table, inspecting a map by the glare of a bare lightbulb hanging from the center of the ceiling.

"Much of the country has never been surveyed. This is the best we have," said Colonel Tekle.

"Not much detail there," Durell said.

The young lieutenant who would pilot them looked dubious. He was only now being told his mission.

"It's treacherous flying country," Ineyu said. "Crosswinds, downdrafts, cliffs over two miles above sea level." His voice was strained, his cheeks hollow. The flame of illness was in his eyes.

"We could hardly map crosswinds in any case," Tekle said softly.

"What's the route?" the pilot said. He crushed his cigarette in a steel ash tray. His hand was steady.

Ineyu stabbed the map with a finger. "Northeast from here until we cross the north fork of the Belesa tributary of the Tekeze. Then due north into the foothills of Mount Rasadajan, about here."

Durell said: "We will depend on Ineyu and Miss Giroud to guide us by landmarks, when we get into the vicinity." He glanced at Deste; she nodded, her eyes quiet.

The fox-faced colonel sucked in a long, hissing breath. "Be warned. If the French have been in on this from the beginning, I can tolerate it. But they should have sent someone else. Miss Giroud has blood ties to the *makuannent*, the nobility. Personally, I do not trust her."

"You have no choice," Durell said.

"No?" Tekle turned to Ineyu. "Watch her carefully," he said.

He withdrew a piece of paper from his blouse pocket and dropped it onto the map. "This is a list of supplies I have requisitioned for you. It includes woolen jackets and boots, if you choose to wear them. Otherwise you will go dressed as you are.

Durell quickly scanned the inventory. It included M-16 rifles; .45 caliber Colt pistols with holsters; knives; sleeping bags; food for two days; spare ammunition; twelve hand grenades; transmitter; medical kit; canteens; waterproof matches; paraffin stove; flares and smoke grenades to mark a landing zone for the airborne troops who would follow.

"It looks comprehensive," he said.

"Very well," Tekle said. "Now: you will establish your base as near the castle as feasible. It is the best landmark in the area. When you have determined the exact location of Ambaw's headquarters and the hideout of this Della Gatta, radio us for the strike. You will act as a blocking force to keep the Italian and his men from reaching their helicopters. When we have subdued the monarchists, we will move against Della Gatta. An airborne platoon will be on alert status, waiting for your call. Your supplies are already in the aircraft. Any questions?"

From beyond the walls came the voices of a ground crew as they made the last-minute checks on a CH-47 helicopter. Durell looked at Ineyu, then Deste. She shoved her hands into the tight pockets of her trousers.

149

The gesture was incongruously male. Her pewter eyes were flat, unread.

"Let's get on with it," Durell said.

The twin-rotor Chinook was high above the fog now. Beyond the windows the pearly banner of distant mountains shone under a brilliant moon.

Durell crouched on the floor plates and checked his M-16 and Colt automatic, slipping a loaded clip into each. Deste and Ineyu joined him. Ineyu coughed and wiped his everted lips with the back of his hand. No one spoke.

Durell tested the edge of his broad-bladed knife, then hooked its scabbard onto his webbed holster belt and clasped the belt around his waist. He slipped his arms into a jacket and returned to his seat to lace up his boots.

Far below a mountain ridge diked a shining ocean of clouds that stretched back toward Gondar as far as the eye could see. The weather was clear in the Semiens. The serrated landscape rose up under them as they maintained their altitude. The silver ribbon of a river gleamed from a dark valley. Durell's stomach seemed to move and he realized the pilot had turned to a new compass heading.

He sat quietly, only vaguely aware of the thin air in his relaxed state. There was nothing to do but wait. Thoughts of his youth on the old sidewheeler, *Trois Belles*, of home, as much as he had, impinged on him. He put them out of his mind. Now was no time to dwell on what might have been had he chosen a conventional career and sired a houseful of children. You did that kind of thinking when all was safe and well and distractions could not threaten your survival. Durell was content with the path he had chosen in any case.

The Chinook lurched into a breathtaking fall, caught its footing, then bounded abruptly skyward as the cold Semien winds asserted themselves.

The pilot called Deste and Ineyu into the cockpit. From here the last leg would be guided by their eyes.

The buffeting increased in violence. Durell saw moonfrosted ramparts all around. Toothed ridges and old volcano cores alternated with dark gorges and valleys.

Sheer canyon walls loomed on both sides as they beat their way up a long valley.

The floor of the valley rose and the helicopter approached a swayback ridge. It slowed and climbed the last steep slope, shuddering and bucking in the wind a few yards above the ground. Then they were hovering on top, the pilot sweating as the wind pushed and tore at the controls.

Deste hurried back to Durell. "We'll have to throw everything out and jump. The pilot won't touch down in this gale," she shouted.

Ineyu was heaving sleeping bags out the door. Durell tossed ammunition and provisions after them. He grabbed the transmitter and jumped to the tufted grass six feet below, rolled and came up in the stinging dust, the tremendous wash of the twin rotors beating at him. The Chinook sank almost to the rocky soil as Deste and Ineyu leaped free, then veered crabwise away from them. A sudden glacial gust rocked it, and a rotor tip thudded into the ground. The helicopter cartwheeled and slammed its nose into the earth in a geyser of stone and dirt. The turbines screamed. There was a flash near the forward engine nacelle and the Chinook roared into a heap of wind-shredded flames.

"The pilot . . ." Deste said.

"It's no use; he never knew what hit him," Durell said.

He turned away, the transmitter still in his arms. The wind soughed through the canyons and burned his cheeks with cold. It thrashed giant heather trees in the orange radiance of the fire. Half a mile down the ridge the black pile of the castle stood out of the rocks.

Durell wondered if Geza Della Gatta walked its ramparts with mad dreams of power.

"We'd better stow this stuff in a hurry. That fire is visible for miles," he said in a taut voice.

They found refuge under overhanging rocks downslope from the wreckage. A few feet away was the verge of an abyss, bottomless in the night. A thunderstorm flayed the ridge just before the first light of day. Fine spray coated them as the air filled with mist and flared with lightning. Then the wind died. Small, rusty clouds scabbed the dawn. From all around came the high calls of shepherds, the bleat of goats. Then the sinister rattle of horses' hooves; shouts of men searching for them. They came perilously close, then passed on.

"We'll give it a few more minutes, then move out. Every hour favors Della Gatta," Durell said.

Deste led them along a bounder-choked path where springs trickled among brilliant mosses, then down to a deep stream course. Wattled ibis squawked in nearby meadows. At 12,000 feet their breathing was labored. Ineyu's face was wan. They paused to rest and Durell said, "Are you sure you're all right?"

The Ethiopian nodded, getting his breath.

Deste said: "We can get a look from down there without being seen. She pointed to a basaltic outcropping.

They moved on cautiously until they were about five hundred yards away from the castle. Durell saw that parts of it were in total ruin, the stones scattered about its base. No one was visible there. From the far side a cable car track ran down into the frosty valley. Three gigantic, black Sikorskys, identical to the one Della Gatta had used at Lake Tana, were parked beside its terminus on the valley floor. A dark oval indicated a cavern down there.

"That's the location of his shops," Deste said.

As they watched two tiny figures came out carrying a crate between them, shoved it into a helicopter and went back inside.

"He's packing up," Durell said urgently. "If we could disable those choppers. . . ." He sighted down the barrel of his M-16, grunted, shook his head. "The range is too far. We might unload everything we had and do no serious harm."

"And alert Della Gatta as well," Ineyu said.

"I wouldn't care about that, if we could knock out the Sikorskys. He can't get far without them." Durell squinted into the valley and considered the situation. He was fully prepared to scrap Tekles battle plan, if necessary; disregard the monarchists and concentrate everything on Della Gatta.

Grass rats chirped and he smelled dogrose and blooming jasmine on the ozone-laden air. Griffon vultures and an eagle soared in the cool valley below.

"We'll use the grenades," he said.

"The noise will betray us. Shouldn't we scout the monarchists first?" Ineyu said.

Durell regarded the sturdy man and remembered that Colonel Tekle had ordered him to watch Deste. Was he supposed to keep Sam in line as well? "How far to Ambaw's headquarters?" he asked.

"Two, three kilometers. I'm not sure," Ineyu said.

"It's somewhere beyond that ridge there," Deste said, pointing to the west. "I'd have to hunt to find it."

"We can't take the time," Durell said flatly.

Ineyu shrugged. "Then I'll go for the grenades."

Durell stayed him with a hand. "I'll go," he said.

He clambered up out of the boulders and around a low rock face and sprinted down the deeply eroded stream bed. Seconds later there came the flat slam of a rifle, the waspish whine of a bullet and he threw himself onto the coarse, black sludge beside the stream. Echoes gushed up and down the valleys. Bellowed commands shattered spaces.

Durell scrambled on, bending low.

He halted beneath a lichen-bearded heather tree and rose to peer through its foliage. A frightened klipspringer bounded from its quiet, green shelter. Durell cursed and ducked, gasping for air, heart pounding.

An angry stammering of gunfire chipped at the tree and twigs and bark showered down on him.

He heard a scurrying noise from behind, pressed the selective-fire lever on his M-16 to automatic and swung the muzzle in that direction. It was Ineyu and Deste.

"What are you doing here?" he said angrily.

"Thought you might need help," Deste said.

"Now if they get one of us, they get us all. Damned smart of you," Durell snapped.

"Have you seen them? How many are there?" Ineyu said, his voice suddenly tough.

Durell shook his head. The fierce mountain sun was higher now and its tropical rays dug hotly into his face.

The sweat on his forehead felt icy in the cold air.

Deste carefully raised her eyes above the lip of the stream bank. When she slumped down beside Durell, her face was ashen. "There's at least a hundred of them. They're moving toward us in a line. The *goramsas*, the young warriors, are jumping up and down and stabbing the ground with knives and yelling threats." She touched her upper lip with the point of her tongue.

"If we had the grenades and spare ammunition . . ." Ineyu said.

"But we don't," Durell said.

"They will know every rock and curve in this stream," Ineyu said. "We won't get far in either direction."

It went against everything in him, but Durell unclasped his holster belt, wrapped it around his rifle and made a show of throwing it over the bank so that the advancing men could see.

Deste's face questioned him.

"We won't stop Della Gatta by dying here," he said.

24

Dejasmatch Nadu Ambaw rode down from the line, lordly on a huge, white stallion caparisoned with red and gold tassels. The dark, secretive slots of his eyes sparkled with hatred, and the hammer chin, now grizzled with beard, was thrust forward sternly. He wore crossed bandoliers, with the Walther P-38 pistol, a white cotton *gabi* looped over his shoulders and a blue scarf tied in a turban about his head.

Four men followed on foot, carrying iron-tipped olive wood fighting sticks and FAL rifles. The rest of his band was armed with a mixture of firearms old and new: Enfields, Carcanos, Mausers, M-16s and FALs.

Ambaw looked down silently. His horse snorted and pawed excitedly; he sat the animal with expertise. His four retainers gathered up the discarded weapons before he spoke.

He directed his words to Deste and Ineyu: "You come here armed, with that man?" He pointed at Durell. "You came in an army helicopter. You have deceived me."

Neither of them replied. He once had taken them for allies; now he knew the contrary. There was nothing to say.

"Come," he commanded. He returned to his warriors, and the four retainers escorted the prisoners in the dust behind the main body.

They followed the gently inclined ridge to its junction with a broad mountain spine, then went west for some distance around the head of a box canyon and came out onto a tablelike ridge that was very wide and sharp-edged, like a mesa.

One of the men up front toppled to the ground. The others gathered around him, muttering and bewildered. The man writhed and clutched at his belly.

"It's the *zar*. Stay away from him or it will get you," Durell heard someone say.

They left the stricken, vomiting casualty to die or survive on his own.

Ambaw's mountain quarters were less than palatial: a squat, rectangular building of eucalyptus and mud with a tin roof and glassless windows. It was at the edge of a village of stone huts plastered with crumbling mud, roofed with thatch over knurled tree heather branches. All around were barley and potato patches and barren, worked-out earth spotted with nettles.

Then Durell saw the size of Ambaw's troop encampment.

There were over a thousand men here—hundreds more than Tekle had expected.

The airborne platoon would be massacred.

Durell read the same thought in Ineyu's bloodshot eyes as they waited in front of Ambaw's quarters. The wind stirred dust from thousands of feet and hooves, and a hubbub of voices boiled from the sprawl of varicolored tents.

Then they were escorted inside, where men sat on low

benches around the whitewashed walls, rifles and fighting sticks between their knees. Fresh grasses muffled their footsteps on the hard-packed dirt floor. Serving women with heavy, swaying breasts bulging under their robes crouched in a corner, whispering and pouring *talla* for the men. The smell of the freshly cut grass mingled with the odor of sweat-stained bodies, the pungent aroma of coffee beans roasting on a flat iron pan.

Ambaw sat in a large chair in the far corner, where he could see everything, his feet on a thick, handwoven wool rug, a servant standing at his side. He glared arrogantly at the three prisoners.

"What is your purpose here?" he demanded.

"We're after Geza Della Gatta. We know he's at the Sinigaglia site," Durell said.

Ambaw did not hurry to answer. His lips twisted bitterly as he regarded them. A serving woman stirred the roasting coffee beans with a twig and poured a few drops of water on them. The water sizzled and snapped.

"The army sent you to spy on me. Why else would you come in a military helicopter?" He nodded, pleased with his reasoning.

"Turn your back on the old ways, *Dejasmatch* Ambaw," Ineyu said. "The world changes. You cannot stop it."

"An amnesty might be arranged, if you help us against Della Gatta," Durell said.

"You intrude in my mountains, then dare to haggle with me? I'll have no dealings with those *lebas*, those thieves in Addis Ababa, except on my terms. They will beg *me* for mercy. As for *Signor* Della Gatta, I have pledged him my protection."

"How can you condone the evil he's doing?" Deste said.

"There is no evil in anything that will serve me," Ambaw said flatly.

"I doubt that some of your men would agree. They and their families are dying of radiation sickness because of Della Gatta," Durell said.

"Yes, it's true, unfortunately. In their ignorance they believe it is an evil spirit, a *zar*. *Signor* Della Gatta made a mistake there, but he won't repeat it. Most of us will survive. Soon he will be gone."

"I suppose he will leave some of his horrible devices for your use," Deste said.

"Of course," Ambaw replied. "When he leaves here, he will deliver one to my agents in Addis Ababa. It will explode at the military government's headquarters there precisely at noon tomorrow. After that I will deal with the leaders of the regime—if any are left—from a position of irresistible power."

Deste and Durell exchanged glances.

The woman had pulverized the coffee beans in a wooden bowl and boiled them in a kettle. Now she handed a cup of the brew to Ambaw, bending from a distance as if to hide her presence. Ambaw sipped the coffee and hardened his face. "Now, tell me—what are the army's plans?" he said.

No one spoke.

Ambaw nodded and his four retainers came forward. "Beat them," Ambaw said simply.

The iron-tipped sticks thrashed through the air. Lightning bolts of pain ripped across Durell's shoulders, ribs, kidneys. A blow whirred at his face and he caught it with his forearm, then dropped to the floor, rolled into a ball and shielded his head with his hands, waiting it out. Pain clamped his mind in an ever-tightening vise, but there was a steellike sanctuary there, a solid nodule of disciplined purpose that torment could not penetrate. He concentrated all his being in that small, detached space, hearing the distant animal sounds of his punished body, the gasps and cries of Deste and Ineyu.

Then it stopped.

Durell raised himself on all fours and saw angry welts across his arms and knuckles. Ineyu moaned and was slow lifting his face from the grass. Torn skin on his forehead dripped dark blood over an eyebrow. Deste's body shook with sobs. Grass stuck to her wet cheek; a red blossom spread through her tangled golden hair.

Durell looked from her to Ambaw and felt a murderous rage. He made no move against the nobleman.

"I do not enjoy this," Ambaw said stonily. "Is the

army planning to attack? When? Tell me and you will die quickly and mercifully."

"We don't know anything," Durell said.

The beating began again.

The torrent of pain, the intermittent questioning, might have lasted fifteen minutes or an hour. It swept away all comprehension in its tidal flood and left Durell groping through a red haze of agony. But he had learned by training and experience how to rise above physical suffering and he was only grateful that no bones had been broken, no vitals ruptured.

They were dragged from Ambaw's dwelling, across a bare, rocky field and thrown into a hut. Durell heard a heavy timber drop across the outside of the plank door. Then it was quiet. Ineyu lay where he fell, racked with spasms of dry retching. His forehead was hot. He drew back his lips, gasping for breath, and Durell saw that blood coated his tongue and gums.

Deste said: "They hit him in the mouth." She daubed his lips with the torn flap of a sleeve.

"There's no bruise or broken flesh—it's radiation sickness," Durell said.

"Is there anything we can do?"

"Nothing. He should be force-fed sugar and protein. If we had our medical kit with us, we could give him antibiotics to control infection. Most of all he needs transfusions of whole blood. He's bleeding inside."

Ineyu opened his eyes. His breathing was heavy, but he seemed to feel better. He said: "I must have crossed the path of the fallout somewhere after leaving Tessema at the wrecked airplane. I was very sick before I left here—maybe I went into shock, I don't know. But when I got past that, it was not so bad."

"The first onslaught is often followed by a period of relative well-being," Durell said.

"And then?" Ineyu said.

"It can go either way."

Half an hour passed. Just long enough so that the raw nerve ends had begun to quiet. Then they took Deste.

Fury mounted in Durell, suffocating him, bursting against his ribs. He saved it for Della Gatta. The Italian's image glowed satanically in his mind; its glare shadowed all else. At noon tomorrow he would turn Addis Ababa into hell—and that would be only the first of many. Durell's patience fed on the knowledge that he must complete his mission. There had to be a way.

He rolled it over and over in his mind.

When they returned with Deste, they carried her. They threw her to the floor. She lay unmoving, like a broken, cast-off doll.

The two men grabbed Durell roughly. He knew he could splinter them both, but he remembered also that a thousand guns waited just outside—and hope for his assignment, for innocent bystanders all over the world, lasted only as long as he lived.

He looked at the retching Ineyu, now spitting up bloody bile, and thought of the stricken warrior abandoned on the way here.

"Wait," he said in Amharic. He dipped his chin toward Ineyu. "Look at him. He has been touched by the *zar* that sickens your people. He has contaminated me and the woman—you'd better look out."

Durell felt their grip on him grow uncertain. Horror darkened their eyes as they backed toward the door, turning him loose.

Ineyu spoke through bloody lips: "The *feranji* who lives in the ground, over there beyond the ridge—he brought the *zar* here, but your lord protects him. What kind of men are you to follow such a one?"

Almost before Durell knew it, the door slammed.

The men were gone.

Noon came and went without food or water.

The hut heated like a kiln under the implacable hammering of the sun. Sweat filled the creases of Durell's cheeks and neck. Deste's strength had returned; Ineyu's nausea had passed for the moment. They sat on the floor, and when they moved, bruised muscles flinched in protest.

Apparently word had spread as Durell intended, and Ambaw could find no one willing to enter the hut for them. From time to time, the dark, weather-beaten faces of tribesmen hovered beyond the small window and squinted at them, trying to see inside without daring to come too close. When that happened, Durell would tell them: "The sickness is *Dejasmatch* Ambaw's doing. He has allied himself with the devil."

As the hours passed and no one entered, he felt better about their chances. He sensed that he was in a struggle with Ambaw for the minds of the superstitious mountaineers. He had no way of knowing where it would lead, but it was better than the sticks or a bullet in the back of the head.

He had a hunch the matter would be resolved soon.

One way or another.

Then, about two o'clock, the heavy plank door scraped open.

"Ato!" Deste drew in a surprised breath as she saw the man with the golden earring and shining, close-cropped head. "And Mitiku!" A taller man with heavy, lidded eyes and somber mouth joined Ato. Durell recognized the two who, with Deste, had helped him escape from the Eritrean village two nights before.

They did not come through the door.

"I thought you had returned to your families," Deste said.

Ignoring that, Ato said, "Come out. We will take you away."

Durell felt hope rise in him, but he was skeptical. "What about the others? Won't they stop us?" he asked.

Ato shook his head silently. Mitiku said, "Some would, perhaps. We will avoid those. Others want to be rid of you; they fear you will taint them with the sickness. Hurry."

Deste scrambled to her feet. She spoke to Durell: "They are casting us out. It often happens in the mountains. It's the only way they know. Let's go."

Durell held back. It was too easy. Deste had said she'd had to pay for their help before; he wouldn't trust them to take his shorts to the laundry. But he had been waiting for an opening of any kind. He suspected this was all he would get. He stood up and brushed a flea from

160

his wrist and looked at Ineyu. The Ethiopian Central lay on his back, cheek bones gleaming below sunken, listless eyes.

"I can't go. I can't make it," Ineyu breathed.

"We'll carry you—get up," Durell said.

"No. I want to stay."

"Then they'll kill you and burn your carcass," Durell said bluntly.

Ineyu beckoned him and he bent over the man, seeing a fire light in his eyes as he whispered: "You must get Della Gatta, and you can do that without me. As long as I remain here, I am poison to *Dejasmatch* Ambaw; yet his men don't dare to lay hands on me. And all the while, I remind them that their leader has betrayed them."

"Don't expect anything to come of that," Durell said.

Ineyu smiled thinly. "Don't *you* be such a pragmatic westerner, Sam Durell. Now go."

Durell rose to his full height. Livid lines showed through rents in the sleeves and back of his shirt. For a brief moment he gazed down at Ineyu. When his time came, Sam thought, he only hoped he could die with the conviction of purpose that now shone on Ineyu's face.

He turned and went to the door with Deste, not looking back.

Confusion clouded the faces of Ato and Mitiku, but they did not press the matter with Ineyu. They, too, refused to come through the door.

There was no challenge to their passage as they skirted the main encampment. A plank of cloud shrouded heights to the north. Its brightness startled the senses. Nearer, flocks of choughs and chats flew over confetti-strewn fields of red-hot pokers, violets, buttercups and scabious.

Durell's thoughts were on Della Gatta when he heard the snap of a rifle's safety.

25

Durell did not have to think. His reaction
came from the gut as he spun on the ball of one foot
and threw a karate kick at the barrel of Ato's rifle. He
took the man completely by surprise. The shiny FAL
clanged and sent a bullet harmlessly into the azure sky
as it was torn from Ato's grasp. Durell crossed the space
between them with a stride and slammed the heel of his
right hand into Ato's chin, hurling him into Mitiku.
Mitiku's rifle hammered and a gout of stone and dust
erupted at Deste's foot as she lunged for him.

Ato ran for his weapon and Durell tackled him.

Deste and Mitiku grappled for his rifle, then Deste
fell backwards and the heavy-lidded man tumbled over
her with a short yelp, the FAL still between them. Deste
wretched the weapon free and axed him in the forehead
with it.

Ato fought with desperate fury, flailing his fists in
wild panic, and Durell just avoided the gleaming thrust
of a curved dagger. He chopped Ato's wrist, glimpsed
the knife spinning away, then buried the point of his
right hand into the man's gut beyond the first knuckle.
Ato made a squeaking noise and went to his knees, and
Durell clouted him with the back of his hand and knocked
him sideways. Durell pressed him against the ground, his
forearm across the wiry stem of Ato's throat. The man's
lips rolled back. His peppery breath blew in Durell's
face.

Durell increased the pressure against Ato's trachea,
threatening to crush it, and the man's mouth gaped wide
and his breathing made a cardboard sound and his feet
drummed on the ground. Then his eyes clouded.

Durell chose not to kill him, but got up and held Ato's
rifle at waist level, covering the two men as they regained

their senses. Mitiku held his head with both hands. Ato rubbed his bruised throat.

Deste sighted Mitiku's FAL on its dazed owner and Durell saw lethal intent on her face.

"Hold it," Durell said.

She glanced at him in perplexity and made a sharp sound of impatience. Then she shouted at the two men: "Why? Why did you want to kill me?"

Ato, on his knees now, spoke tremblingly. "*Dejasmatch* Ambaw said you would bring the army to destroy us."

"He ordered you to kill us?"

"No—he said we should not kill you; not until he has made you tell the army's plans. But then no one would go into the *tukul* to fetch you for him. He was very angry. The men discussed it. They wanted to kill you so that you could not bring the army, but not in the camp. They were afraid to handle your bodies to dispose of them, afraid the touch would give them the sickness. They made us take you away to shoot you. They thought you would go with us, if no one else."

Mitiku sat up. Durell saw that his eyes were clear now. A lanner falcon swooped low over the grass and tried to bowl over a rat. It missed and arched high into the breeze.

Durell said: "Listen to me. You are wrong about the sickness. Look at us—we have been near Ineyu a long time now, but we are still strong, as you have seen. The sickness is not catching. Only those touched by the dust of the devil's light get it. If Ambaw had not permitted it, there would have been no devil's light and no sickness. Now he protects the man who did this to your people. You go back and tell your comrades that."

The two men struggled to their feet.

Durell heard whoops in the distance. He glanced toward the camp. Men were coming on foot and horseback.

"They must have heard the shots—they're coming to finish what Ato and Mitiku started," Deste said.

"May we go now, lord?" Ato's voice was a supplicating whine.

"One more thing," Durell said. He lifted his rifle menacingly. "Protect Ineyu."

The two nodded hastily.

"Hide him and take care of him."

"Yes. Yes, lord."

"Swear it."

They nodded again. "Yes, we will," Ato said. Durell saw a bloody rip in his ear where the golden earring had been.

"Swear it on St. Michael."

The two men exchanged nervous glances. They believed a dead man's soul was escorted to heaven by St. Michael on the right and Satan on the left. In heaven each claimed it and argued until the soul was weighed in a scale. If St. Michael refused to do his part, there could be no hope in the afterlife.

Durell aimed at Ato's head. "Swear by St. Michael or meet him right now," he barked.

"I—I swear it. By St. Michael," Ato said.

"I too," Mitiku said.

"Go!"

The men ran, *shammas* flapping in the wind, until they were small, white figures. A ragged wave of shouting tribesmen came toward them.

The igneous rock of the cliff face was cold and gray where Durell and Deste picked their way across windy ledges and inched down treacherous chutes. Durell had chosen to start down an almost vertical bluff as the quickest way out of sight. The descent was too sheer and too far to try for the bottom without climbing gear. Once they were down a hundred feet or so, all he asked was luck enough to cross horizontally and connect with the detritus of an old rock slide. Compared with the cliff face, it would be a stroll down its conical side to a lower ridge that descended easily to the valley floor. Meanwhile, overhanging ledges sheltered them from discovery.

Deste paused and lowered her eyes, then clamped them shut with a frozen expression.

"Don't look down," Durell said. He moved to grasp her arm and stones clacked and snapped, bouncing away into space. The wind blew a fine net of hair across her cheek. "Just keep your courage up. We'll try to cross the valley and reach the transmitter on the next ridge. We've got to signal Tekle and tell him he'll need more men," Durell said.

Deste nodded at the stone wall an inch from her small, aquiline nose.

They moved crabwise along the cliff, carefully planting each toe and finger before taking a step. Durell envied the poise of the walia ibex that bounded away almost on air. Across the shadowed valley a herd of baboons fed near a saw-toothed outcropping that gleamed under the mountain sun. Miles away veins of sparkling snow swooped toward the ice-capped peak of Mount Rasadajan. The breeze brought the smell of balsam with the shouts of irate tribesmen.

Relief trembled through Durell's arms and thighs as he stepped onto the rockslide and hurried on skittering stones toward a growth of giant heather where he intended for them to rest.

A flock of thick-billed ravens exploded out of the shaggy trees, cawing in alarm.

Durell yanked Deste's arm and ran on past the grove.

"Sam! I'm winded!" she gasped in a strangled voice.

"We've got to keep moving. If we don't stop Della Gatta, Addis Ababa goes up in smoke tomorrow at noon," Durell said urgently.

She dug both heels into the loose debris and sat down. He looked at her angrily. She wiped at the sweat filming her brow. "I can't," she said.

Durell was sorry for her. He could not expect her to have his stamina. But he told himself that nothing was going to stop him now. He had come too far; Della Gatta was almost in his grasp. "I'll have to leave you," he said.

"Just—just one minute—for a breather."

She smiled unexpectedly and he felt things shatter in him—pleasant, expendable things. His being carried many such shards and fragments, many regrets.

"No. They must have heard the crows. They're just up there." He shook his hand loose from Deste's and started on down.

The noise of her stumbling, lurching descent came after him.

Somehow she had found the will to go on.

They were beyond the slide and on the slope of the lower ridge when gunfire erupted, dragging a chain of echoes across the mountains. The men were shooting from the edge of the mesa, at least a thousand yards away. They wasted ammunition at an impossible range, and Durell did not bother to take cover, but staggered on down with Deste, legs leaden in the oxygen-starved air.

Perspiration shone in the corners of his eyes as he looked back. Horsemen galloped back and forth as they sought a way to ride down. Men on foot spilled onto the rockslide and scuttled down it with breakneck abandon, yelling and whooping.

Durell saw the nearing canyon floor as a jumble of enormous boulders. Here and there stands of scraggly eucalyptus and cedars bent in the valley wind. A plummeting stream threw the sun's glare into his eyes. He regarded the scene, intent on finding the quickest avenue of escape. Over to the left was something unnatural about the lay of the rubble—something disturbed.

He angled toward it.

The guns racketed closer behind them. The cries were louder. Slugs hissed through the air and dusted the stones. A glance back and Durell realized he almost could distinguish the faces of his pursuers. Deste was slowing him dangerously, but he would not leave her yet.

He dashed through the clutching torrent, then scrambled through a shelter of boulders up the incline of the next ridge. Deste leaned against a house-size block of stone and her breath came in sobs. She pointed up ahead. Durell shielded his eyes against the intense glare above with a flattened hand.

A dark line of horsemen trotted along the line where the mountain met the sky. They had galloped around the gorge to cut off their flight. As Durell watched, they began picking their way deliberately down toward him.

26

Durell's gaze swept the valley. Sweat dripped from his chin. The men who had followed were close behind now, and the horsemen methodically closed the gap ahead.

"We're boxed in," Deste said.

"I don't think they have us pinpointed. We'll break for those trees over there. Use the cover of the rocks and maybe they won't spot us." He motioned with his head, and Deste scrambled away. He was at her heels as she rounded a jagged outcropping and crashed into a dense stand of eucalyptus saplings. Orchids spangled the grove in colors of royal purple and pale, waxy yellow. Durell heard the *ping* of bullets among the boulders they had left. The mountain men had not seen them come in here.

Hauling himself from trunk to trunk, Durell clambered up the abruptly steepening slope. The trees were rooted in loose stone, and he fell to his knees as rocks slipped from underfoot. Durell suspected from their sharp-edged uniformity that they were mine tailings, but he had been unable to see a shaft from across the valley.

He paused, breath rasping, and peered through the branches. The leaves in the grove pecked on the wind. A finch twitted. From below came the steady flushing noise of the stream.

He began to worry that he had been wrong.

Then relief stunned him.

Dead ahead lay a dark cavity, easily overlooked. The opening had collapsed and a hole only a yard in diameter remained to mark the entrance. Durell crawled inside, heedless of serval cats that could be lurking there. Deste lay beside him, panting, hands quaking with exhaustion. A chain of coarse sand spilled briefly from between the rocks at her elbow.

When her breath quieted, she sighed deeply and said: "It doesn't look good, does it, Sam?"

"We've made it this far. Just be thankful for small miracles." Slowly and quietly he released the clip of his FAL, drew back the bolt, ejecting a live round, and blew dust from the receiver. He wiped the round on his pants, thumbed it back into the magazine and inserted the clip back into the rifle. He would use the weapon with reluctance; he did not want to give away their position.

The confused noise of men's voices came from down below. They might already be among the trees, Durell decided, but he could not see them. He heard the hollow clack of horses' hooves nearby.

Deste said: "There's no hope of reaching the transmitter now. Do you think Tekle will come anyhow, if he doesn't hear from us?"

Durell shook his head gravely. "We can't expect Tekle's help if we don't get to the transmitter. If our pilot hadn't been killed, he might have led the troops in. As it is, there's no way for Tekle to find us. Even if he did, he wouldn't stand a chance with only a platoon."

"And do we stand a chance, Sam? Two of us against all of them?"

"Maybe not. I can't let that stop me." He felt a squirm of worry in the pit of his stomach.

Deste regarded the blue-black pits of his eyes, the grim set of his jaw. "No, you wouldn't," she said.

"Della Gatta's choppers are the key. Destroy them and he's stranded—Ambaw's bomb is stranded."

Deste sighed. "You frighten me a little, Sam Durell. Would you have left me, up there on the mountain?

"Yes."

Deste's brows lifted very slightly, then settled. That was all. She turned her face toward the trees and said: "You might as well have left me. This has become a suicide mission."

Durell kept his ears tuned to the sound of movement down below. "It makes a difference to me where I die; what I die trying," he said evenly. "You can sit it out here. You could hold off an army for quite a while."

"No, I'm coming with you."

"You're sure you want that?"

"I'm sure."

Durell touched her shoulder gently. Then he got to his feet, sore and tired. "First, I'll check out this tunnel. Keep the entrance covered."

He moved cautiously along the rock-strewn floor. Ahead the darkness was complete; behind, the oval of light marking the entrance grew smaller and smaller. Durell was puzzled. The shaft was as straight as a gun-barrel. There were no side tunnels or pits. He thought perhaps it was dug straight into the mountain to intersect the slant of some mineral-bearing stratum or maybe a quartz-encased ribbon of gold. He glanced back and the patch of sunlight looked like a hand mirror. He turned his face and the green image floated on his retinas.

His toe struck a large stone. He stepped over it into heaped rocks, leaned forward, reached out and found rubble piled before him like a wall. He clawed his way up a bit and found only more of the same. He pushed a breath of frustration through his nostrils.

The rattle of gunfire echoed down the corridor.

Durell ran toward Deste, aware of slugs whining between the stone walls. Dust rolled about the opening as the tribesmen focused their firepower on the entrance. Durell heard the frenzied hammering of automatic weapons. Bullets slapped and screamed, and he threw himself to the ground and scrambled forward on his belly.

Then Deste screamed, "Sam!"

He felt as much as he heard something give way in the mountain. The floor shuddered and a distant rumble made the skin prickle at the back of his neck. Shrieks of terror came from outside and mixed with the other noise, and then savage, earth-rending thunder packed the tunnel with shock after shock.

Abruptly all was deepest night.

A million cicadas whined in Durell's ears, the only sound. Dust choked him and burned his eyes as he staggered to his feet. He groped ahead in a dreamlike unreality, as if floating through a nightmare of nothingness. He hoped for the merest pinprick of light, but there was none. The entrance was completely blocked by the landslide. Utter isolation in the heart of the mountain brought an electric surge of anxiety. Nothing had prepared him for such catacylsmic violence from nature itself.

"Deste?" he called. The unseen walls mocked his voice.

"Here, Sam."

He breathed more easily. "Where?" He groped on.

"Over here."

He heard her stir; his fingers grazed her hair. Deste found his hands and pulled him down beside her. "I thought—the rest of the tunnel . . ."

"It held. You weren't harmed?"

"No, I heard it coming. Did you find anything back there?"

"Looks like it's blocked by an old cave-in."

They sat in silence, neither voicing the hideous forebearings uppermost in their minds. They could expect no rescue. The hours could stretch into days, the days into a week or more. But eventually this stygian chamber would become their tomb—while Della Gatta put the rest of the world to the atomic torch, beginning with Addis Ababa only hours from now. A desperate urgency lashed at Durell, and he started to rise.

"What are you going to do?" Deste's voice seemed loud in the inner stillness.

"Start digging," he said tersely.

"Oh, Sam! You know it's hopeless. That isn't just rubble from the mountainside there. The roof of the entrance came down. There are blocks of stone that must weigh thousands of kilograms."

"There's no point in just sitting here."

She tugged on his hands. "I'm frightened; put your arms around me," she said.

He did as she asked and she kissed him on the cheek and said: "Can we forget for a moment, together?" She arched her rich, full body against him, and he responded to the warm, yielding pressure of her curvature in spite of himself. Her lips were wet and supple as they kissed, her breath rapid and strong on his begrimed face. There was an avid hunger for life in her voice as she moaned:

"Love me, Sam, darling. Make it the way it was behind the waterfall—only more."

She made a small, pinched sound of surrender, and Durell gathered her into him.

"Hey, Cajun!"

They sat back from their shattered embrace.

"It's Hennessey!" Durell said with disbelief.

27

Durell heard the bearlike movements of the big man who came down the corridor, but he could not see him. He picked up his FAL.

"Sam, damn you! Are you in here?"

He seemed to be alone. "Straight in front of you," Durell called.

The shuffling came nearer; a stumble and a curse; coarse breathing. The glance of fingertips. "Oh. There you are."

"Keep back," Durell said.

"What? You worried about me since I've been with them?"

"I don't trust you, if that's what you mean."

"That's okay; you figure they worked on me. I'd be the same as you." Durell could sense his immense bulk before him, lines of force emanating from it.

Then Hennessey said "Listen, they're a tough crowd, boy. I'd've had the dickens getting away if it hadn't been for you. They're in a tizzy. Ambaw sent a runner to tell them you were on the loose. I guess they just sort of stopped thinking about me."

"How the hell did you get here?" Durell demanded.

"Well, there was only one way to go," Hennessey said. "Della Gatta's works is in an old highway tunnel the Italians started. They never got to finish it, because of the war. I guess Della Gatta knew about it and that's why he came here. They had me back toward the rear—

171

the place is cluttered with all kinds of equipment and instrument consoles—even spare engines. Must have taken him months to haul all of that stuff in. Anyhow, I wasn't very well guarded. I guess they figured there was no place for me to go. And I couldn't have got out the front—no way. When all the ruckus started about you, they were jabbering and running around, and I just sidled back to the end of the tunnel to see where it went. I found this little crawl space, and here I am. I just about died when I heard that landslide."

"Sam! There's a way out!" Deste cried.

"Who is that?" Hennessey said blindly.

"It's a long story," Durell replied.

Hennessey had solved the mystery of the long, straight shaft they were in. It was what mining engineers called a pilot drift—a small tunnel excavated to explore the geology of a rock mass through which a highway or railroad tunnel was to be carved. The main tunnel had connected with it from the other side before work stopped.

"How did you know we were in here?" Durell asked.

"I didn't, but when the crawl space opened up and I knew I might have reached the other side of the ridge, I thought the chances were good. I'd heard gunfire and decided I'd better call ahead—you're not a good man to trip over in the dark."

Durell stood up, uncertain of his balance in the total blackness. The pile of rubble a few yards to his left made a splintering sound and a boulder thudded to the floor. Durell smelled a fresh wave of dust and heard debris rattle as it continued to settle.

"Sounds like this place is ready to come down around our ears," Hennessey said.

"You'd better show us the way out," Durell said. He found Deste's hand and hauled her to her feet, the FAL saddled in the crook of his other arm.

"Maybe we can get back before I'm missed. You have weapons, don't you?" Hennessey said.

"Yes," Durell said.

"Good. It won't be easy, getting out of Della Gatta's rat hole. Give me a gun. I'll lead the way."

"You stay between us. I'll take the gun," Durell said.

172

"Okay, Cajun. Whatever you say."

They felt their way to the heaped stones that Durell had supposed blocked the end of the corridor. Only inches beyond where he had ventured was a cramped stone shelf. The low ceiling scraped his back as he crawled to the rear wall. There he found a hole about two feet in diameter, the opening out of the stone duct traversed by Hennessey. Far ahead a yellow disc of light beckoned. The passage was empty.

Durell struggled along on rock-bruised knees, the FAL cradled in his right arm, the action kept free of grit. Hennessey's breathing labored behind him, resonant in the narrow space. He could not hear Deste.

Durell stopped, peered cautiously ahead. The mouth of the tunnel was an arm's length away. There came the throb of machinery, probably gasoline-driven generators, Durell judged. The lighting beyond was a low, soft radiance. Stacks of crates blocked the view. Shreds of excelsior littered the floor, which was covered with stream gravel for drainage. A couple of crates were labeled *acqua minerale*, mineral water. Most were unmarked. They might contain anything from potatoes to plutonium.

Durell did not relish the prospect of entering the main tunnel. The cramped opening of the drift blinded his vision on every periphery. Hesitantly, he edged his head out.

Something crashed against the back of his skull.

In the last pained instant of consciousness the image of the landslide ripped across his mind and he thought the mountain had fallen on him.

Then there was nothing.

Something stung Durell's cheek.

He swung out of darkness on a giant pendulum and heard a murmur of voices as if through a wall, then swung back and the light and the voices receded.

Another sting, the sound of a slap against his cheek.

He opened his eyes and saw a dark, intent face move back. Above the man's head was the arched roof of a prefabricated building; behind him the last rays of the sun beamed floridly.

"Get up, Mr. Durell; you've rested long enough," the cold, familiar voice of Geza Della Gatta said in English. There was low laughter, then an expectant silence.

Durell rose slowly from the straw-covered floor. A headache drummed at his temples. Before him a long table almost filled the room. A couple of lanterns glowed amid the food there, the table laden as if for a banquet.

Some twenty men sat around it, all eyes on him. They must have come from all over the earth to judge by their features and dress.

Directly across from him sat Della Gatta, his rivet-like eyes malevolently on Durell. Cesari, seated on his right, glared at him like a hungry ferret. Ambaw sat smugly beside the Corsican.

On Della Gatta's left sat Mira Seragate, her almond eyes troubled with apprehension.

Durell did not have to be told then that she had betrayed them to Della Gatta on Degas Island, and anger roweled him.

"What have you done with Deste Giroud? Where's Tom Hennessey?" he asked.

"They are elsewhere. They will be amenable to my plans with you out of the way. You are like a tree that will not bend with the wind. Therefore, you must snap in two and die."

Della Gatta's reptilian eyes were unblinking, and Durell thought of the Biblical snake that had first brought death to mankind.

"You expect them to call off pursuit, then," Durell said.

"Exactly. We depart within the hour. Everything I intend to take has been loaded aboard my aircraft. There will be a brief stopover in the hills, outside Addis Ababa tonight—to deliver a weapon to agents of my friend *Dejasmatch* Ambaw—then on to a base in a new country where the officials will ask no questions."

"There are nearly a million people in Addis Ababa," Durell said.

"Is that an appeal to my emotions? I expected better of you."

"A psychopath has no emotions," Durell said flatly.

174

"I'm appealing to your reason, if any is left. Do you think you can slaughter whole populations and get away with it?"

"Yes." The black eyes narrowed slightly.

Durell heard the wind draw a sericeous noise from the arched roof of the hut. He smelled the reek of kerosene thrown off by the lanterns. "Why did you bring me here?" he asked.

"Merely to give my friends and clients the pleasure of seeing you die. They represent the Red Star; the Movement for Tribal Autonomy in Africa; Pan-Nazism; nationalistic fronts from half a dozen countries—even the Authentic People's Union from your own United States. They will take the tidings of your death—along with small nuclear devices—to their comrades. They will spread the word that Geza Della Gatta is supreme."

"Is that all you stand to get out of this? It hardly seems worth the effort," Durell said.

Della Gatta hunched his vulturelike shoulders more closely; an obscene smile crossed his bony face. He turned to Cesari and said something under his voice. Durell watched as the Corsican gave his MAB pistol to Mira. Her hand was small and white around the massive black grips.

Then Della Gatta said: "Miss Seragate shall have the honor. She has proven her loyalty. This is her reward." He looked at her and said in a bored voice:

"Kill him, my dear."

28

Mira came slowly around the table, her eyes wide, almost trancelike, her rich lips parted over gleaming teeth. She did not take her gaze from Durell as she approached from across the room.

Della Gatta said: "Don't go too close. That's far enough. He's quite desperate now."

Mira stopped, facing Durell and slightly to his left. The candle flame in her irises focused to bright points of light and Durell felt his throat harden and his tongue go dry. So it had come full circle, he thought. He was back to the beginning: a beautiful girl with a gun; his life in the scales.

Hope now was foolish.

She had been faithless all along.

Mira raised the gun toward his face. Her knuckles looked bloodless on its handle. Her lips trembled, and Durell tensed to lunge at her.

Then, in a blur of motion, she began to fire wildly.

They erupted in a ducking, yelling frenzy as shot after shot slammed into flesh and walls. Everybody was scrabbling for his weapon. Cesari tumbled Della Gatta beneath the table and dived after him. Ambaw's head rocked violently as the top of his skull disintegrated in bloody spume.

Durell did not wait to see what would happen. In an instant he bowled over his astonished guard and hurled himself toward the door. Out of the tail of his eye he saw a muzzle flame tongue from among the confusion of men and Mira went down.

Beyond the door he sprawled a second guard onto his back, sent a looping kick to the temple and heard bones crunch under the toe of his boot. He swept up the man's FAL and triggered a short burst at the doorway. An Asian in a western business suit pitched across the threshold, his Nambu automatic thudded into the dust.

Durell ran through the twilight, aware now that he was within the crumbling walls of the old castle. Nothing but heaps of stone remained to mark the former buildings. The only structures standing were Quonset huts set up by Della Gatta.

He scrambled over a pile of mud bricks and sprinted toward a V-shaped break where copper daylight shone through the black line of the wall. He started through the breach and sucked in a startled breath. A couple of feet beyond was the verge of a chasm hundreds of feet deep.

The men had topped the rubble; their bullets puffed and clanged all around him. He leaped through the opening onto a narrow stone shelf and took cover behind the wall. The chill breezed sucked at him as if to hoist him over the precipice. He leaned toward the break, his finger tightening on the trigger in a quick, sharp burst. A loose file of men darting toward the castle gate threw themselves to the ground. Durell figured they would try to get him in a pincers outside the wall. He looked over the edge of the cliff and the wind blew back strands of hair across his eyes. Sweat trickled down his ribs. There was no way down.

He estimated twelve to fourteen rounds remained in his twenty-round magazine. The men inside kept him away from the break with a withering fire. He expected some of them were advancing toward the break under its cover. He hunched low and waited, jaw set in a hard, straight line, his mind cool and clear. All he could do when the final assault came was to take as many of them with him as possible. The death of any one of them might mean the salvation of millions of people, at least temporarily.

He heard the clamor of gunfire sputter out and waited for them to storm the breach. He pointed his rifle toward the opening and tensed his finger.

But no one came.

Five seconds passed, then ten, and he sensed a tinge of alarm in shouts coming from inside the wall.

The distant, whooshing echoes of gunfire came across the mountain crags. Durell looked back up the ridge. Hundreds of mountain tribesmen rushed toward the castle ruin, an amber horde in the last light of day.

A dozen languages babbled frantically inside the wall. Durell peered in and saw the last of the men running out through the gate. He stepped quickly to the middle of the breach and the FAL jerked and jolted in his hands. Two men screamed and fell as a long spray of slugs smoked into the stone around them.

Then the huge wooden gate slammed shut, leaving an eerie quiet as night closed over the sky.

The tribesmen flooded inside and made way for Durell as he rushed to Ineyu, who sat astride a chestnut stallion. A thread of concern tugged at Durell as he regarded the unsteady form of the square-shouldered man. Ineyu looked more ill than ever; only an iron will had kept him in the saddle.

Ineyu said thinly: "Ambaw's men mutinied. They overcame their fear of me to get revenge on Della Gatta. I've already radioed Colonel Tekle. Ato and Mitiku are out there on the ridge. They will set flares when they hear the helicopters."

He grinned weakly and slid into Durell's arms.

The place was a bedlam as the tribesmen whooped, fired their rifles into the air and smashed windows in the huts. Durell rejected the idea of trying to form a party to bring Della Gatta to bay. He told two men to help Ineyu into the dining hut, and also to see to the woman in there; not to harm her if she were still alive. Then he stuffed his pockets with clips of 7.62mm ammunition, his hands trembling with urgency, and pushed his way through the throng and out of the gate.

The cold sky glowed with crystal stars. Hyenas barked among the immense ridges and valleys. Durell felt his way carefully around the hazardous perimeter of the wall to the cable-car landing. He found a donkey engine running, a windlass slowly spinning as Della Gatta and whoever survived with him descended toward the valley floor.

Down there the giant S61-Ls waited, laden with instruments of mass destruction.

Addis Ababa could not escape because of Ambaw's death.

Della Gatta would go through with that out of sheer madness. And what would be next? New Delhi? The Hague? Washington?

Durell hurried to throw the winch into reverse, but before he reached the gear lever, a voice heavy with menace said: "No further, *m'sieur.*"

He stopped and looked for Cesari in the shadows of night.

"We will wait a little while, eh?" Cesari said. "Otherwise I must kill your colleague. It's always a shame to kill a pretty woman."

Durell saw then that Cesari held Deste as a shield a few feet beyond the windlass.

Durell stood on the rocks like a dark colossus in the night, feet planted widely apart, the breeze fluttering his torn clothing. The donkey engine chuffed on, sending Della Gatta closed to escape.

"Throw down your gun; they're leaving without you," he said.

"True. But wait a bit, my friend. Give it only a short while, and you and Miss Giroud will still be alive, and I shall be *your* prisoner. I am a mercenary soldier; I know when to fight and when to surrender. First I must provide my employer with a rear guard; then there will be no dishonor in laying down my arms. My reputation will be secure. You see, I must maintain my integrity."

Impatiently Durell realized that Cesari was accomplishing his purpose all to well. Talk was killing precious seconds. He lunged for the donkey engine, heard Cesari's pistol slam and flinched as the bullet exploded against metal, showering his forearm with hot needles of lead. Deste turned on the Corsican and they scuffled for his gun. Durell pressed the engine's kill button.

A second later, Cesari looked up into the muzzle of Durell's rifle. He raised his hands and his grin glittered golden in the light of the rising moon. He said: "I have done the best I could. . . ."

His head jerked to the side, and Durell heard the ripe thud of a bullet, the clang of a shot. Cesari's grin warped shapelessly and his body bounced down the mountainside.

Durell's eyes raised to the jagged ramparts of the castle. He saw no one there.

"Get Cesari's gun and come on!" he called. Deste obeyed quickly, golden strands of windblown hair twisting about her face.

Durell wondered how much time was left—ten minutes? Five?

He slung his rifle and scrambled down the steep slope, thankful for the unobstructed path of the cable-car track. He almost collided with the abandoned car near the valley floor, dug in his heels and sent stones skittering on down. He paused there for an instant, instinctively expecting the noise to bring gunfire. Then he plunged on, deciding they must already be aboard the helicopters. The valley was cold; the smell of frost was in the air.

Abruptly the wide, level space of the helicopter pad took shape out of the darkness, and Durell's eyes focused on three elongated shapes, each dimly luminous with the green glow of cockpit lights.

Brilliant white and blue flame shot from turbine exhausts; long rotor blades twisted slowly and gathered speed. Durell shouldered his FAL and sighted as best he could. The three giant Sikorskys bounded into the air all at once. Durell pressed the trigger and held it down until the clip was empty, feeling the weapon buck against his shoulder. Fire blossomed on the twin turbine nacelles of the nearest craft before it could make headway.

Durell tossed the empty clip away and inserted a new one, aware that Deste was beside him now, taking aim. Both fired at once. A dart of flame spurted from one of the remaining two helicopters as they headed up the twisting valley.

The first craft lost power rapidly. One side was a fiery tatters. It limped across a sheer abyss, spun on its axis, then crashed onto a stony spine some fifty yards away. The screams of its occupants came clearly through the night.

Then, incredibly, the shape of a man staggered into the doorway, narrow, hunched shoulders dark against the roiling inferno behind.

It was Geza Della Gatta.

His hands gripped a blunt little submachine gun. Its snout flickered and bullets choroused angrily where Durell and Deste sat exposed by the fireglow.

Durell took careful aim and his gun racketed against his eardrums.

Della Gatta danced crazily and reeled into the jaws of darkness.

The two remaining Sikorskys were beyond a turning miles up the valley when an electric flash whitened the mountain walls. The enormous light, tinged with violets and blues, outlined every hill and ravine up there, then a writhing fireball hurtled skyward. The noise of a thousand cannons rebounded and clashed among the trembling Semiens, and every direction responded with the rumble of landslides. Up and down the valley, plumes of dust lifted into the moonlight, dwarfed by the shining mushroom to the north.

In the unearthly silence that followed, not even the hyenas made a sound.

"The bomb must have been set off by the fire in the second helicopter," Deste said in a subdued voice.

"Something went wrong. We'll never know what," Durell said. "With all the plutonium scattered around up there, they'll have to quarantine the area for a long time."

Deste sighed and got wearily to her feet. "I guess that wraps it up, Sam."

Durell looked back at the castle. He wished with every tortured fiber of his being that she was right, but he had to say, "Not quite."

The mountain men were getting drunk now, celebrating the end of Della Gatta with *talla* beer made by their women. They milled about an enormous bonfire that consumed everything they could haul from the huts. Rifles banged at the sky. Horses reared and neighed. The explosion in the distant reaches of the valley had horrified them, but Ineyu had calmed them, saying the cloud containing the *zar* was blowing away from them and soon would dissipate. Durell made a mental note to suggest that the radioactive track of the fallout be surveyed by air so that any villages caught in its path could be decontaminated.

No one seemed to mourn Ambaw. Colonel Tekle was likely to have no trouble rounding up whatever leaders remained in Ambaw's disorganized encampment, Durell decided.

It was of little consequence to him one way or the other. He was very tired, and he had one thing to do before he rested.

He wanted to get it over with quickly.

The men carved the meat of an ox and ate it warm and raw in the traditional way, dipping the slivers into fiery red pepper paste. He pushed through the throng and found Hennessey perched like a boulder atop a pile of rubble near the break in the wall. He was grinning pleasantly as he watched the scene. The orange glow of the bonfire made his face look like copper. A *gabi* covered his head and shoulders. Beside him lay one of the FAL rifles.

He waved when he saw Durell, and said: "Hey, Cajun!"

Durell stood at the edge of the mound of stones and looked up at him without expression. "Come down. I want to talk," he said.

"Sure!" Hennessey started down.

"Leave your rifle there. You won't need it." Durell held his own FAL casually.

Hennessey hesitated; something besides the bonfire's reflection glinted in his light blue eyes, but the smile remained. He left the rifle and came down in big, crunching strides.

"Hey, goddamnit, we did it, Sam! It took some luck, but I always say you make your luck, right? When I think what might have happened if I hadn't led you out of that tunnel. . . ."

Durell stepped back, beyond the big spade of a hand Hennessey offered.

"Hey, what's got into you?"

"I said I want to talk. Let's go over there, where it's private." Durell motioned toward the broken wall with his rifle.

"What's to talk. It's over!"

"Are you coming?"

The grin disappeared. "Whatever you say, Cajun."

"You first."

"I don't like your tone." Hennessey looked surly as he stood his ground.

"Go," Durell said, raising his rifle slightly.

Hennessey gave Durell a measuring stare, then shrugged his shoulders. "All right," he said.

His back looked immense as Durell followed him through the breach and out of sight of the other men. Hennessey sat on his haunches on the narrow shelf of stone. The nearly full moon was sharply defined, its light brilliant in the thin air two miles above sea level. The hood of Hennessey's *gabi* cast a black band of shadow across his eyes. Tiny flakes of gold, the firelight of a village, shone in the middle distance. Moon-dappled clouds crept up the valleys. The breeze brought the scent of herbs from mountain moors.

"What's eating you, Cajun?"

"Why did you kill Cesari?"

"Is that all you're sore about? I didn't think you had a chance to see me. You looked pretty busy."

"I didn't see anybody. I knew it had to be you. The man had surrendered."

"So what? He was the scum of the earth. I figured he'd only slow you down."

"You were afraid he would talk," Durell said evenly.

"Those are strong words, my friend. You're not as smart as I thought to bring me out here and say something like that. It's a long way down." Hennessey nodded toward the brink of the gorge.

"How much did Della Gatta pay you?"

"You're talking like a crazy man."

"Where's Tessema?"

"How should I know? Somewhere in the U.S., I guess."

"He never made it there—our embassy checked for me. I contacted it from Gondar last night. That was when things started unraveling for you, Hennessey. Last night."

Hennessey did not reply immediately. He looked thoughtful as he tapped a cigarette from a pack and placed it between his lips. Still sitting on his haunches, he half-turned out of the wind and bent over a match in his cupped hands. He flipped the burning match into

183

the chasm. Durell watched carefully, his finger loose on the trigger of his FAL.

Then Hennessey said: "Tell me your side of it; then we can talk it over." The cigarette burned quickly in the fresh breeze.

"All right. Here it is, as much as I can piece together. You've worked both sides from the beginning. You agreed to keep a lid on K Section's investigation until Della Gatta could finish up here and duck out. You knew it would take only a week or so, and it seemed simple. But everything was predicated on the supposition that I was dead, and you were the only agent involved. When I turned up, things started to sour. Instead of sitting on your hands, you were forced into a more active role—you had to start taking real chances, but the money must have made it seem worth it."

"You haven't said anything solid yet, Cajun. If you've got it, let's hear it." Hennessey puffed on the cigarette and tossed it away.

"When Deste arrived at the safe house in Gondar, she carried orders addressed to you, Hennessey. They should have been addressed to me, as the chief field agent. When I called the embassy about it, I found that you had never reported me alive. Yet you spent half the night in Asmara on line with K Section to get the Sinigaglia file. Such an oversight could only be intentional, and there could be only one reason for it.

"Yeah? What's that?"

"You could kill me with impunity as long as I was already dead to K Section."

"What about the airstrip; we were in that together."

"You knew I'd head for Tessema the first thing. He hadn't mattered until I returned from the dead. You fixed it with Cesari to look like you had been overpowered, and he had got away with the pilot. But I arrived a minute too soon and blocked Cesari's exit. He took the opportunity to get rid of me. You were expendable, but he knew you would understand that—it's that way in our kind of world. You let him take your gun for effect; if I'd given you mine, as you requested, you would have killed me then and there.

184

"You did everything to strengthen the illusion that you were playing it straight, just in case I survived. You joined Della Gatta at Degas Island, but you stayed out of sight. You played the Judas goat in the tunnel today, but you came unarmed, thinking I would trust you that way—I expected trouble when we came out of there, but it was the only hope Deste and I had. Even when Della Gatta had me in the hut here tonight and things looked their darkest for me, you didn't tip your hand. You knew K Section too well to chance getting on its kill list."

Hennessey rubbed his face with his hands. "They know all of this back in Washington?" he asked.

"Enough. They know about Tessema; they know you kept my survival a secret from them."

"Geez, look at us here." Hennessey sounded tired. "Maybe we're going to kill each other, and for what? Della Gatta's dead, the bomb threat is gone. Everything is cool. Sam, I've been sick of this business for a long time. It's no way to build a life for yourself. No home, no family; just danger and death, killing and more killing."

"Cut it out. You enjoy it. You killed Tessema in cold blood. Admit it. You shot Cesari down when he was helpless. Had Della Gatta paid you off?"

Hennessey nodded his massive head. "It's all safe in a little Swiss bank. He wired it there and gave me a receipt. A million smackers—would you believe it?"

"Durell said: "That money's going to draw interest for a long, long time, Hennessey."

"We could split it down the middle. We could disappear, maybe to Java. That's a beautiful place. I've got friends there. Lord, how I could use a nice rest."

"No deal."

"You going to kill me?"

"It's your choice." Durell's face was a grim mask. "You can have that rest in Leavenworth, providing the local authorities don't hang a murder rap on you before I get you out of the country."

"I'll have a smoke and think that over. There's no hurry, is there?"

"No hurry," Durell said.

Again Hennessey withdrew cigarettes and matches from a shirt pocket. The cold wind leaned against Durell's back. Beyond the broken wall, the tribesmen reveled as noisily as ever. The bonfire cast a yellow nimbus above the black ramparts. Far up the heather-strewn ridge bright red flares suddenly sparked to life, one by one, as Ato and Mitiku marked a safe landing zone for Colonel Tekle's airborne force. Durell felt no compassion for Hennessey, only revulsion for the deaths he had caused, the incalculable carnage he would have helped to loose. The bitter taste of betrayal filled his mouth as he considered the cardinal rule of his lonely way: trust no one.

Hennessey's face and shoulders were twisted half away, hands cupped near his lips. He seemed to have difficulty lighting a match in the wind. He bent closer to the ground.

Then the right hand lashed out with snakelike speed.

A grapefruit-sized stone hurtled toward Durell's chest.

He dodged, aware that a misstep would send him plummeting into the abyss, and hit the castle wall just as the rock crashed into his left shoulder, numbing it. Hennessey uncoiled explosively, hands reaching for him, lips skinned back in a snarl.

Durell's rifle staggered in his good arm, the noise shattering, the muzzle blast flickering on the ancient stone wall. Dust puffed from Hennessey's shirt front and his jaw gaped, but he did not go down. For a nightmarish instant, Durell barely avoided the huge, flailing hands. Then Hennessey hurtled past with a bloody gurgle, white, dead eyes in his face, and crunched headlong onto the stone shelf.

Durell drew a deep breath and touched his bruised shoulder. He glanced through the breach. The shots had gone unnoticed amid the clangor of celebrating rifles there.

As he had hoped, there had been no interference, no witnesses.

Drained of all emotion, he gazed briefly at the corpse that lay half over the rim of the gorge. He put his toe against it and braced himself against the wall.

Then he nudged it over the edge, into the windy vastness below.

29

Warm, sweet-smelling showers nursed

the highlands around Gondar as Durell and Deste walked out of the base dispensary. The fog had lifted and the moon wiped scudding clouds with silver. It was almost midnight and the small military installation was quiet. An army doctor had examined them and swabbed their lacerations with germicides and told them they had suffered no serious harm.

Now they were free to go their separate ways.

They did not speak as a staff car sped them to the little British-built Beagle Husky that would fly Deste to Djibouti, her home base in the French territory of the Afars and Issas on the Gulf of Aden 400 miles east. The car halted beside the twin-seater and Durell saw the prop turn reluctantly until the engine fired, then whirl to a flashing mist.

He looked at Deste across the rear seat. She held her small, beautiful frame in a posture of reserve. Her noble blood asserted itself in the outthrust point of her chin, the straight lift of her slender neck. She tucked a golden strand of hair into place and said: "You've been marvelous. I guess this is goodbye."

Her eyes shone full of moonbeams, and she looked down at her knees.

"Next you're going to want to shake hands."

"Don't be unkind. I must make my report in person."

"The job comes first, always."

"I suppose we won't meet again."

Durell made no reply. The driver stood beside Deste's open door.

"Well, goodbye," she said.

"Goodbye."

Durell took a long, soaking bath in the Iteghie Menen Hotel, then strolled the short distance to the safe house, awakened old Koidakis and spent half the night encoding and filing reports to K Section via Cairo Control. Sometime in the early morning hours the Greek called him to the telephone, awe-bloated eyes enormous behind thick spectacles. Durell stood holding his fourth mug of steaming coffee as he placed the receiver to his ear.

"Are you all right, Samuel?"

Only one person called him *Samuel*: General Dickinson McFee, the boss of K Section. "Yes, sir. As well as could be expected of a Lazarus, sir," Durell replied.

"Your reports seem to be coming in at rather a slow pace. Are you fatigued?"

Durell knotted his jaws. "No, sir. I slept three hours night before last."

"I gather we nearly blew this one. I regret Hennessey's perfidy," McFee said discreetly.

"Do you, sir? He was two years overdue for recall to Washington and psychological reevaluation."

"We couldn't spare him from his post. We need more personnel. Would you like to have a permanent station in the U.S. and take over recruitment?"

"I wouldn't recruit any Hennessey's, sir."

"You sound annoyed, Samuel."

"Sir, the next time I'm killed, I don't care who you send if you make sure I'm dead first."

The overseas connection crackled and whistled.

"I'm reading your reports as they come in. I'll brief Sugar Cube within the hour. I just wanted to congratulate you and tell you to expect new orders shortly," McFee said.

"How shortly?"

McFee hesitated. "I suppose I can hold them back for a couple of days, maybe a week if a certain situation deteriorates no further. We'll let it ripen."

"Yes, sir. I hope you'll let it get very ripe, sir."

"Goodbye, Samuel. Get a good rest—as soon as you finish your reports."

There was a click as McFee hung up.

Closed shades blocked the late afternoon sunlight from the hospital room. Durell had no thought of his own aches as he stood over the unknowing form of Ineyu. The man's everted lips, flaked with chapped skin, were slightly parted. His broad chest rose and fell with shallow breathing as plastic tubes dripped whole blood and glucose into his arms.

"His condition is critical," said the white-clad nurse.

"Then it can go either way?"

"His condition is critical, that's all I can say." She left the room, closed the door behind her. Durell looked around. There were no flowers or messages, no symbols of caring in the sterile room.

He stood silently for a long moment, feeling useless.

Then he took paper and pencil from a drawer of a steel bedside table and wrote: "Get well soon. Highest regards. Durell."

He left the note propped against Ineyu's unused water glass.

Durell entered another room a few doors down from Ineyu's.

"Sam, baby! I'm glad you came. Ow, it hurts to move." Mira reached out with her good arm and took his hand. She was wan, but looked all the more beautiful for it. Her lustrous almond eyes seemed to take up half of her face. A nurse had brushed her hair, and her mouth shone wetly under new lipstick.

"Thanks for what you did, Mira," Durell said gently. "You're lucky you weren't killed."

"If you could call being shot through the shoulder and arm lucky," she said. "Look, I wanted to tell you: I never tried to hurt you, Sam, even when I had the chance. Believe me?"

"I don't know," Durell said.

"When I saw what Della Gatta really was—what he was really doing—with my own eyes. . . ."

Durell nodded wordlessly.

"I'm through as Sheba, right, Sam? I can see it in those beautiful, dark eyes of yours."

"We can't use you anymore," Durell said. "They want a statement for the files at K Section. Tying up loose ends."

"Okay, Sam. Della Gatta was after Ineyu, because he had seen the atom blast, so he had my place in Asmara staked out in case Ineyu tried to reach me. Ineyu never came, but Hennessey did, the first night you were missing. After that, Cesari got to him at the Ras and made a deal—all Hennessey had to do was sit tight and do nothing until Della Gatta had his project wrapped up and out of the mountains."

"Then the next day I surfaced alive at the Ras," Durell said.

"Yes. Hennessey knew Cesari had planted a bomb in your car, but he wasn't taking any chances. He came back to involve me in his cover-up scheme when I still thought you were dead. He accused me of murdering you to protect the monarchists. He said no one in K Section would ask questions if he eliminated me, but that he would give me a choice. I could work for him and Della Gatta and make a lot of money in the process—something like $100,000. I was scared, but I really wanted that money."

"So you said all right," Durell said.

Mira nodded. "And Hennessey bashed in my transmitter—he said he had already disabled yours. The worst moment came when they threw that hand grenade at us in your hotel room."

Durell said: "Hennessey must have called Cesari and told him I had returned there. He had no way of knowing you were there, too."

"I figured they thought I was getting too chummy with you. I just wanted to run, and you were handy to run with. I thought I had to do something to get back into Della Gatta's confidence, so I let him know about your meeting with Ineyu on Degas Island."

Durell heaved a deep sigh and loosened his hand from Mira's.

Mira smiled, earthy and provocative once more. "I wish we could have got together, Sam, baby."

"Maybe you'll come to the U.S. to see Uncle Joseph sometime," he said.

"You're just saying that. Uncle Joe won't tell me how to find you, will he."

"No," Durell said.

Mira's smile was tight. "Take care," she said.

"So long, Mira."

The *Addis Zemen* carried a page-one story that day about the monarchist defeat. It quoted Colonel Mamo Tekle extensively. There was no mention of Della Gatta and his terrible project. Nor of Durell, Deste, Mira or Ineyu, of course. An editorial commended Tekle on his "brilliantly conceived and masterfully executed" attack. The *Zemen* avoided mention of the Special Branch, and referred to Tekle as an airborne brigade commander whose star was sure to rise.

Durell figured the story signaled the beginning of a play by the secret police chieftain and his supporters for more power behind the scenes.

He folded the paper in his lap, sitting on the tall, thatched veranda of the Iteghie Menen, long legs crossed, a bourbon and soda in his hand. He was conscious of the pleasant sounds from the dining room behind him as he regarded King Fasiladas's ancient castle through a trellis heavy with bougainvillaea and bright with small birds. The sun was going down, coloring the clouds pink and gold. He suddenly dreaded spending another night in the land of the deposed Lion of Judah.

There was nothing to hold him here.

He decided to leave.

The thought restored a sense of purpose to the day. He went to the lobby and called Tekle's office from a public phone booth. If the colonel would make space available on a courier plane to Addis Ababa, Durell could leave that night and catch a commercial flight from the capital city to the U.S.

Tekle was not available at the moment.

Durell asked that the colonel return his call as soon as possible and went to his room.

The twilight brought the hues of a tiffany lamp

191

into the room as he waited beside the telephone in a brocade-upholstered arm chair. From the wide gardens below his window, full of flowers and brightly blossoming shrubs, came the cooing of pigeons, the warble of green and red lovebirds.

Durell's thoughts were far away when a small sound nudged his mind. In a long-formed habit, his hand found the new Beretta automatic under his arm, and he looked up.

A wall mirror in an ornate rosewood frame revealed a person's silhouette backlighted in the door of the adjoining room.

Durell took his hand away from the gun.

The intruder clearly was unarmed.

The light from the other room filtered easily through a gown of sheer, white silk, outlining the contours of beautifully tapered legs, ripe, willowy body.

"I hadn't expected you," he said to the mirror.

"I came back on the chance you would still be here. I'm on holiday now," Deste said.

Durell felt his pulse quicken as she glided toward him in the dusky room. When she was in front of him, all golden and lovely, he rose and took her in his arms. For the first time, this was no escape from terror, no refuge in desperation. When Deste surrendered to his embrace, it was with all the magnificent poise of her noble lineage. But now there was no reserve.

Her lips moved to his ear, and she whispered: "How long do we have?"

"I'm awaiting orders," Durell said huskily.

"I can give you some." She pulled him toward the bed. "Come here, my darling."

Durell obeyed.

A few moments later the telephone rang.

And rang.

And rang.